Upgrade

The High-Tech Road to School Success

Claudine G. Wirths & Mary Bowman-Kruhm

Illustrations by Ed Taber

Davies-Black Publishing
Palo Alto, California

Also in this same series by these authors:
Are You My Type, or Why Aren't You More Like Me?
Choosing Is Confusing: How to Make Good Choices, Not Bad Guesses

Published by Davies-Black, a division of Consulting Psychologists Press, Inc., 3803 E. Bayshore Road, Palo Alto, CA 94303. 1-800-624-1765

Copyright 1995 by Davies-Black Publishing, a division of Consulting Psychologists Press, Inc. All rights reserved. No part of this book may be reproduced, stored in a retrieval system, or transmitted in any form or by any means, electrical, mechanical, photocopying, recording, or otherwise, without written permission of the Publisher.

99 98 97 96 95   10 9 8 7 6 5 4 3 2 1
Printed in the United States of America

Library of Congress Cataloging-in-Publication Data
Wirths, Claudine G.
   Upgrade : the high-tech road to school success / Claudine G. Wirths & Mary Bowman-Kruhm ; illustrations by Ed Taber.
     p. cm.
   Includes bibliographical references (p. 111).
   ISBN 0-89106-069-3 (alk. paper)
   1. Study skills—Juvenile literature. 2. Educational technology—Juvenile literature. 3. Computer-assisted instruction—Juvenile literature. 4. Study environment—Juvenile literature. [1. Study skills. 2. Computer-assisted instruction.] I. Bowman-Kruhm, Mary. II. Taber, Ed, ill. III. Title.
LB1601.W57   1995
371.3'028'12—dc20
                                                                       94-33802
                                                                             CIP
                                                                              AC

First edition
      First printing 1995

Contents

Quick Reference Guide

v

Introduction:
What's New With You?

vii

Chapter One
No Cupcakes on the Keyboard

1

Chapter Two
Booting Up Your Study Aids

11

Chapter Three
Getting Together What You'll Write

33

Chapter Four
Saying It With Style

47

Chapter Five
Backing Up the Facts
61

Chapter Six
Downloading and Speaking Up
79

Chapter Seven
Anyone for Pi?
87

Chapter Eight
Taking a Byte Out of Tests
97

Chapter Nine
Your Place in High Tech
107

Selected Resources
111

Acknowledgments
113

Glossary of High-Tech Terms
115

Quick Reference Guide

Use this Quick Reference Guide to help you with the skills you're looking for.

Skill	Chapter
• Get acquainted with computers	1
• Improve your reading	2
• Improve your work in math and science	7
• Keep a journal	3
• Write a 1- to 2-paragraph paper	3, 4
• Write a book report	3, 4
• Write a short story	3, 4
• Write a research paper	3, 4, 5
• Prepare a speech	3, 5, 6
• Study for a test	8
• Organize your studying and assignments	2
• Take better notes	2

Introduction: What's New With You?

The top CD? A digital phone? The latest electronic game? If you're the kind of person who's always on the lookout for what's new and better, then we wrote this book for you. You are probably already using the latest high-tech equipment for fun because high tech offers so many new and interesting possibilities. Have you considered using this equipment for schoolwork for the same reasons, or are you still studying and doing your assignments the way you've been doing them since the first grade?

Young people who are still fussing with ballpoint pens and lined paper are missing the advantages of incorporating computers and other electronic magic into every school subject they take. You don't have to be one of those kids!

In this book, we'll talk about how to use today's high-tech gadgets and gizmos and the latest findings on the way people learn. These ideas can make your schoolwork easier and a lot more interesting! We'll show you some tactics for using computers, camcorders, tape of your assignments, too. With a little effort on your part and the information in this book, you can soon get the hang of using high tech, and we predict that you'll see big improvements in the way you study, learn, and write. We also predict you'll see a super change for the better in your grades.

Sound interesting? Then read on while we talk with another young person about how to make the high-tech information age work for you.

1
No Cupcakes on the Keyboard

Welcome to the twenty-first century! Your generation is the first one ever to have access to all kinds of high-tech equipment. It's available in your schools, at home, and throughout your daily life. We wrote this book for someone like you who can see the advantage of using these technological wonders not only to have fun, but also to improve your schoolwork. As a consequence, your grades should climb up as well.

Is this book going to tell me how to run a computer or camcorder?

No. We leave that to you because there are so many different kinds of models on the market, and your equipment may be different from ours. What we will do is tell you how to take advantage of the special benefits offered by high-tech equipment. And all this will help you slay the homework dragon and improve your grades. But introducing you to the various high-tech bells and whistles that are out there now isn't all this book will do. We'll also suggest ways to help you actually improve the way you learn.

Are you talking about the same old thing my teachers call "study skills"?

*Study skill*s is a term teachers have used for years to refer to study methods. Most likely, your teachers have shown you the same study skills they were taught. Learning in today's and tomorrow's high-tech world, however, demands new approaches to studying and learning.

If you use a computer, even just for games, you know that when new games and **software** come along, you want to upgrade what you have. We want to show you how to upgrade your old study skills, too, by replacing them with new learning tactics that incorporate high tech. We'll also help you personalize these tactics so that you can develop your own study system, one that works best for you and will help you as you move through school.

These learning tactics can become the basis for lifelong learning. In the twenty-first century, the best jobs will go to those who have the skills to keep up with the latest developments in technology and ideas. But that's for much later in your life. Let's look at ideas you can use right now.

Sounds okay to me.

We'll start by talking about computers. In this book, we will use a lot of terms you may not be familiar with. As you become computerwise, you will need to understand them to get the most out of your computer and this book. To help you, we have listed these terms in a glossary in the back of this book. Glossary terms appear in bold-faced type for easy identification the first time we use them, like the term "software" above. Whenever you come across a bold-faced term that you don't understand, refer to the glossary. If you still don't understand, ask the computer expert in your own family or at school. Everyone who uses a computer effectively has to learn the language sooner or later. In time, these words will roll off your tongue as if you had known them forever.

Do you spend much time with a computer now?

I'd spend a lot more time if I could, but we have only one computer at our house and it seems like everyone in the family wants to use it at the same time.

Why not have a family conference about using the computer? Assign each person a set number of hours a week at scheduled times. A message board where you can write each person's time and name would do the job. Or have a calendar with family events, including computer schedules, pop on the screen whenever the computer is **booted up**. If someone wants more time for a special project, that person would need to schedule extra hours in advance. Swapping times would be allowed only if both people agree.

A computer calendar might work. I'll talk to my parents about trying one.

You will probably also need to set some rules for computer use. Here are a few ideas to get your family thinking:

- Agree that **files** belonging to other members of your family are off-limits to others. Reading someone else's files is like reading their diary or personal mail.
- Don't handle **disks** with sticky, messy fingers; **hard disks** don't drive on that kind of food.

- Keep all drinks and snacks well away from the work area. No eating cupcakes at the computer! Little crumbs of icing (or crumbs of anything else) can gum up the keyboard.

I know. My little brother spilled a soda on our keyboard and it cost a lot to replace it.

Help your little brother learn that a computer is not a toy. A computer is an expensive piece of equipment. The initial **hardware,** including the hard disk, **monitor,** and keyboard, probably cost more than the stove or the refrigerator in your house. By the time you add a good **printer**, some software, and floppy disks, you can double or triple the total value of your setup.

We got a catalog that has all kinds of cool software for our computer, but Dad says the ones I want cost too much.

To prevent breaking the family budget, you have to be very selective in choosing software. Always check with friends, teachers, and the neighborhood expert to be sure the software you're considering is what you want before you buy it or ask for it as a gift. Many times, a simpler (and cheaper) piece of software will do everything you need.

Spend big money only on super software that gives you a major teaching aid in a subject you're having a lot of trouble with. Or maybe some sophisticated software in science, music, or art that takes you wonderful places your schoolwork doesn't or can't would be a good investment.

Remember, buying software is like buying books or CDs—it's a very personal matter. Look at various **programs** and ask lots of questions before investing your money in something you may not need or even find useful.

So far, the only money I've spent on software is on games. To be honest, at school I use a computer a little, but at home, playing games is about all I do on it.

Playing games is fine, but if you only play games on your computer, you're missing a chance to use a valuable tool that can make your schoolwork go easier, faster, and better. Using high-tech equipment properly can put you in charge of those papers and assignments that teachers keep making. However…

Uh-oh. I knew there was a catch. This all sounded too easy.

…until you learn to **keyboard,** it will actually take you longer to do homework on a computer. Sign up for a keyboarding course at school right away, or get some software to teach you. Learning correct keyboarding isn't hard and won't take long. The more you practice, the faster you will get. You'll probably start to **input** into the computer much of what you handwrite now. Soon you'll be turning out sharp-looking papers in a fraction of the time it now takes you.

Before we go any further, let us stress one of the most important habits you must develop as soon as you begin to create anything on a computer. Every few minutes, **save** *what you have done* and, before you stop work for any length of time, *make a* **backup** *copy*. Of course, always make a backup copy of any important files before you **shut down** the computer. We can't stress this enough. We tell you this from our own painful experience of losing some golden gems that are now floating forever in **cyberspace**.

One of my teachers has said we can't use computers for our written work.

Sadly, there are still some teachers who are behind the times when it comes to using high-tech equipment. However...

Uh-oh. There you go again. What's the catch this time?

...there are some good reasons why a teacher may not want you to use a computer for your schoolwork. Since not everyone has a home computer, the teacher may want everyone to have an equal chance to score well on papers that are graded for neatness, grammar, and spelling. Another reason may be that the teacher is afraid someone else may write a student's paper if it's done on a computer.

That's not the only way to cheat with an electronic gadget. Some guy told me how he cheats using one of those little electronic pocket planners.

Anyone who wants to cheat will find a way—even a high-tech way. But we hope you will choose not to use high tech for cheating—not only because it is wrong, but also because you can damage both your future and the whole future of high-tech equipment in schools! As you have already noticed, some teachers are still uneasy about the use of computers and other electronic equipment in the classroom. If they believe students will use them for widespread cheating, they will be even less likely to let high-tech gizmos, regardless of what kind they are, into the classroom.

Well, what can I do about getting my teacher to let me use a computer for writing a paper?

Try telling your teacher why you'd like to use it. Explain the advantages to both of you. Don't try to do this in twenty seconds between classes. Make time during lunch or after school to talk about it.

If several teachers are opposed to the use of computer-generated work, your parents may want to talk with the teachers or the principal. Sometimes teachers need to know that the administration and parents are in favor of a change in classroom procedure.

If a teacher still wants you to do the assignment in a specific way, even if it seems old-fashioned to you, don't forget who gives the grade!

I think most of my teachers will let me use a computer for homework, but I may have a problem with Mom. When we first got a computer, I spent hours playing games. I didn't do anything else. Then she put a stop to that and put a time limit on how long I can stay at the computer, even if no one else wants it.

Good for your mom. Getting so wound up with electronic equipment that you forget to do homework or wash the dishes is very easy. But worst of all, you lose contact with family and friends. No matter how great any electronic gadget is, it can't share popcorn with you at the movies, give you a hug, join you on a bike ride, or listen to what happened at the ball game.

Your mom may also have concerns about your health. She may be worried that sitting at a computer for long periods will cause you to have backaches and eye strain. To remind yourself when to quit, set the timer on the computer. If the computer doesn't have one, the old wind-up kitchen timer is high tech enough for that job. When it rings, chimes, buzzes, or beeps, *stop right then.* If you don't, you'll get absorbed again in a matter of seconds.

Mom also tells me not to sit too close to the computer, but I don't pay any attention to all that talk about radiation.

Listen to your mom. As far as anyone knows, computers are safe, but the monitors do emit radiation, and your body stores up every bit of radiation it receives. Too much radiation may cause you problems later in life. The best advice available today is that you sit a comfortable distance from the screen and avoid spending long periods of time close either to the side or back of the monitor while the computer is running. To be sure, check with your family doctor and take the doctor's advice about how much total time you should spend in front of the TV, the computer monitor, and any other radiation-emitting device. You also may want to check into the possible advantages of getting a screen shield for your monitor.

If a computer is such a time-waster, maybe even a health hazard, and software is so expensive, tell me again why I would want to use a computer for schoolwork!

There are a whole host of reasons that far outweigh any drawbacks. Turn to the next chapter and we'll start talking about them.

2

Booting Up Your Study Aids

As you become competent with high-tech equipment and acquire a high-tech state of mind, you'll discover dozens of ways to combine high-tech power with brain power. But first we need to talk about tactics for learning that will help you take advantage of high tech. One important tactic is to develop a personalized assignment sheet.

Not a homework sheet! They're little kid stuff.

Does your mom or dad keep an appointment book? Or maybe an electronic organizer or planner or computer calendar to help them remember what they need to do?

Well, yes, but that's different.

No, the idea is the same. Your work is no less important than theirs, so you also need some system for keeping track of your life and your "to do's." By writing down those details, you won't need to remember your homework assignment or the date your report is due.

When you design your homework sheet, don't forget to include an area where you can list special materials needed to complete an assignment.

Homework sheet *I* design? I didn't want to have one a minute ago and now I'm designing my own!

Why not? If you design your own, you can create something that is useful to you and your needs. If you find it isn't helpful, you can always go back to whatever you do now. Two sample homework sheets, one daily and one weekly, are included here to get you started. Copy the sheet you like best, enlarging it if you need to, or come up with your own. Some of the following ideas may help you, based on your level of expertise with a computer and the resources you have available, to develop a homework sheet that appeals to you:

- Make a sheet you copy, or design a variety of them that you alternate.

- Make one that looks like a job ticket from an auto shop—or the face of your computer screen. Or an outline sketch of a favorite breed of dog or horse. Or…come up with your own idea!

- Add original drawings from your **paint/draw program** and print them in color.

- Write your assignments inside outline drawings of **clip art.**

- Add space for important events of the week, like a friend's birthday or a big party.

- Add a "To Do" space or a space for doodles.

Once you find or make a sheet you like, decide how you'll use it. Some people like to clip a fresh homework sheet in the front of their notebook every day or week. If that appeals to you, run off multiple copies of your sheet on your printer or photocopy it.

Others like to use the same one over and over by putting it in a plastic jacket and writing on it with a wipe-off marker. Instead of a

Sample Homework Sheet 1

Homework Sheet for Week of: _____/_____/_____

Write down assignments based on their importance to your grade and/or priorities. If an assignment *must* be done, place it in the box; if you feel it is less important or even optional, write it inside the oval.

Monday

Tuesday

Wednesday

Thursday

Friday

Long-Term Assignments   **Due**

_____

_____

☆ **Remember:**

Sample Homework Sheet 2

Homework Sheet of _____
Date _____

Write in your assignments in the boxes below. You can add names of other subjects in the unlabeled box.

English	Social Studies
Science	**Math**
_____	⭐ **Remember:**

marker, you can attach sticky notes if you prefer. "Sample Homework Sheet 2" would be ideal to use this way.

In short, design and use a sheet that will help you jot down assignments, take home the materials you need, and turn in work—both long-term projects and daily assignments—on time.

An assignment sheet in color with some cool drawings would be okay. I could even make some copies for my friends.

That's a great idea. Maybe some of you who live near each other could form your own homework group and use the same assignment sheets with your own logo on them. You could study and work on projects together.

I could use a sheet like that to keep me on track. To tell you the truth, some nights my parents think I've spent two hours on homework, when a lot of that time I've been fooling around.

When you sit down to do homework, begin by booting up your mind as well as your computer. Different people have different ways of doing this. Here are a few ideas students have told us work for them:

- Jump right in and do your easiest or shortest assignment first to give you the feeling of success. But once you have finished it, use the momentum to keep you going. Don't tell yourself you've earned a rest!

- Tackle the hard stuff first to get it out of the way before you get too tired. Take a timed break and then wrap up the rest of your work.

- Set a timer or your computer clock to sound its alarm in fifteen minutes. Get right to work, knowing that when the alarm goes off, you have earned a five-minute break. Then get back to work again as soon as the five minutes is up.

If you are already familiar with the computer, try these suggestions:

- Have upbeat messages that float across the monitor as **screen savers.** Look up some wise sayings of others or create your own slogans, like "Move it!" or "Keep your eyes on the prize."

- Type your top priorities for the evening on a to-do list that appears when you boot up. Sit quietly and review it for several minutes while you clear your mind of everything else.

- Play a word or math game on the computer. Set a timer for fifteen minutes and promptly get to work when the bell rings.

You may think of a better way to get your mind moving. The best learning tactics are those you yourself discover, using ideas from this book and from your teachers, friends, and family. Only you can find your best way.

Sometimes I get started, but then I get blocked by the assignment itself. For instance, if the teacher says I have to read a long chapter in a book, I sort of stare at the pages and flip through them, but I sure wouldn't want to be tested on what I've read.

The job of reading and understanding the context of a great many pages in a limited time can seem overwhelming. Do you ever flip through to the end of the assignment and hold all the pages together to check the thickness, and then sigh?

To get past that type of mental block, think for a minute about how a computer works. You don't give a computer several commands and expect it to sort out what is most important, what should come next, and so on. You give it one command at a time in the order in which you want things done.

When you do an assignment properly, your mind works much like a computer. *Your mind works best if you break the job down into small steps, or commands, in sequence.*

I'm not sure what you mean. Let's say I have to read a chapter from a novel for my English class.

If you're reading fiction, such as a chapter in a novel or a short story, mentally review what you already know:

- Who the main characters are
- Where the story takes place
- What has happened so far

You will then read to find out what future events befall the characters and what impact those events have on them.

Should I read a chapter in my social studies or science book the same way?

Add one important step. If the chapter is from a textbook, you should first preview the material by asking yourself what you can learn by first checking out the things listed below:

- Chapter title
- Graphs, charts, or pictures
- Headings and subheadings

- An introduction and/or summary
- Margin notes

Then, as with fiction, ask yourself what you already know about the subject, and, most important, ask yourself *why* you are reading. No, we don't mean "because the teacher said to." We mean you should consider what the focus of your reading will be. In other words, what should you concentrate on? If you are reading about Africa, for example, concentrating on facts and figures and important historical dates for the various countries on that continent requires a very different way of reading than if your focus is on understanding elements of African culture long misunderstood by Western Europeans and Americans.

Sometimes a teacher will give us questions and say, "Read to answer these questions."

That teacher is helping you focus your reading. Whether you decide what you should look for when you read or use what your teacher gives you, establishing the focus of your reading is an important learning tactic. This tactic sounds obvious, but many students don't understand how helpful reading with a focus in mind can be. Ask the **find function** in your mind to locate what you're looking for, just as you use the find function on your computer.

Am I ready to read now?

Yes. Whether you are reading fiction or nonfiction, the process is basically the same. Read the material. But don't whip your eyes down the pages, slam the book shut, and punch the TV remote or grab the phone. Really reading requires more.

Again, just as when you're using the computer, you should "save" every few paragraphs. You should also check while you read to be sure your mind is "saving." The best software saves automatically. So should you. Periodically stop reading. If the material is complicated, you may have to stop every few sentences. If it's simple, you may read an entire chapter. When you stop, ask yourself:

- What did I just read?

- Did I understand what I read? Reread if you didn't "save" it.

- What's my reaction? How do I feel about what I read?

We've included two charts that can help you break your reading assignment—whether fiction or nonfiction—down into small steps. One is called simply a "Format for Reading Fiction"; the other is a "Format for Reading Nonfiction."

You can photocopy them. Make a new copy of the appropriate chart and fill in the blanks each time you read. You'll have an excellent summary for later use in studying. If you are already using your computer for schoolwork, you may want to copy them onto your computer—a **scanner** can make the job easy.

I can try the charts, but I have trouble learning anything just by reading about it.

Each of us has to figure out how we learn best because the way each of us learns can be very different. Some people, for example, learn best by *doing* or, at the least, by *watching* others doing. Some learn best by *working in a group* with other people. Still others prefer to take in information by *listening*. Others like to *read things through* by themselves, on their own time. What is your best way to learn?

Format for Reading Fiction

Examples of fiction: novels, short stories, plays, fables

Before you begin, ask yourself:
- What do I already know about what I'm going to read?
- What do I want to find out?

Then read rapidly, slowing your pace occasionally, rereading at a *very* fast rate for review to discover the information needed for the Summary Information below.

Summary Information

1. Title

2. Setting—time and place

3. Characters

4. Problem faced

5. Events that happen—rising action

6. Climax—the high point of the action

7. Conclusion—falling action, the end

Format for Reading Nonfiction

Examples of nonfiction: textbooks, encyclopedia, magazine articles, online materials

Before you begin, ask yourself:
- What do the title, chapter headings and subheads, introduction and/or summary, and graphs, charts, and pictures tell me?
- What do I already know about what I'm going to read?
- What main point(s) will I focus on while I read?

Preview quickly to get an overview, then read slowly to note details. Then read rapidly for review to discover the information needed for the Summary Information below.

Summary Information

1. Title

2. Topic

3. Main point(s)

Words to Remember

List only words that are (1) important to the material read and (2) ones you might need to know in the future.

Word and Page Reference	Definition

I'm not sure, but my sister says I'm doing it wrong when I listen to a book rather than read it. For my last book report, I listened to the book on tape and she said if I do it again, she'll tell Mom I'm cheating.

Did the teacher tell you that you were to work on your reading skills?

No, she just gave us a list of books.

Then we don't feel you cheated if you listened to the entire book and not a shortened version of it.

I listened to the whole thing and then I listened to parts of it again a couple of times.

That sounds fine to us. Whenever you use an alternative format of a book, be sure that the version you're using is the same as the original. For instance, a cartoon book will seldom give you little more than a general idea of what the original is about and very few movies or videos are faithful to the book version. A good many books on audiotape—called **audiobooks**—though, are exactly as written. Read the notes on the cover to be sure.

Great. I'm going to try to get all my books on tape if I can.

Hold on! Your sister is right in urging you to read more. Just as you can't learn to shoot three-point baskets by simply watching a video, you can't learn to read difficult material in books or on screen if you just listen to audiotapes. Audiotapes help you learn vocabulary, but the only way you learn to read better and faster is by actually reading.

And why work at reading, you ask? Because reading is how we deal with most of the important information that is worth saving, retrieving, and passing on to others, either on screen or off. The higher you go in school, the more you will be required to read, and you won't always have audio resources, so keep reading in addition to using any other learning tactics you prefer.

I don't know why I have trouble understanding what I read. I don't have any trouble figuring out what's happening when I watch a music video on TV.

Music videos and many commercials on TV pop visual images in front of you. That is a type of reading because what is being said or played emphasizes the images but doesn't explain them. Many researchers are studying how we understand what we take in through our eyes. Some of them believe that such rapid-fire images force you to focus, since the images don't move in sequence from one to another. As the images rush through your mind, you capture the substance of the meaning.

Understanding something that moves in an orderly manner, like what you read on a computer monitor or in a book, is a very different matter.

When I have a lot to read, how can I get it all done—and understand and remember it besides?

Learn to vary your rate of speed when you read. You need to read some things slowly, but many things can be read quickly or even skimmed over. In this book, we suggest reading rates for the three major types of reading material—fiction, nonfiction, and directions. For example, for nonfiction, we suggest you read as quickly as you can when previewing because you are simply trying to get an overview of the material; you can then read slowly to note details. For review, you should again read quickly.

Varying the reading rate is important. You can waste time if you read slowly when reading quickly will get you the information you need. On the other hand, you can also make mistakes if you read something like directions too quickly.

You're right about that. My dad and I made stir-fry for dinner last week. We were trying to hurry and goofed up with some of the ingredients. It ended up tasting a little funny.

Rushing and reading directions are a lethal combination. Directions require a special way of reading, whether the instructions are for baking a cake, making a model, doing a science experiment, or taking a test. When you read directions, your goal is the completion of an end product.

First, ask yourself what you already know. Get out all the tools or equipment or materials you'll need. (In chemistry class, read each step of your lab instructions three times; the life you save could be your own!) Visualize the end product as you work. The "Format for Reading Directions" on the next page summarizes these steps.

When you've finished reading, ask yourself:

- Does the product look and/or work like it's supposed to?
- What's my reaction? How do I feel about the result?

Format for Reading Directions

Examples of directions: software manuals, recipe instructions, board game instructions

Before you begin, ask yourself:
- What do I already know to help me with what I plan to make/do?

Then read the entire set of directions quickly, but then read very slowly as you follow each step, then reread to check for accuracy to discover the information needed for the Summary Information below.

Summary Information

1. Picture/describe the end product

2. Check tools and equipment needed

3. Check materials/ingredients needed

4. Visualize while following steps

How should I read when the teacher asks us to find some little piece of information, like who were the two generals at Gettysburg?

If you want to find specific information, practice using a seek-and-find system.

Seek-and-find?

When you drive through a town where you aren't familiar with the radio stations, you probably use the seek-and-find function of the car radio to locate a station you want to listen to. The seek-and-find function lets you quickly bypass stations until you find one you might want.

Train your eyes and mind to perform this same seek-and-find task when you read to find information you need. Skip over information you don't want until you find what you do want. (Hint: Keep in mind a key word or two. In the case you mentioned, they would be *Gettysburg* and *General*. Let your eye look only for the key word or words.) Then stop there and read carefully what you were **searching** for. If you need to do so, take notes on the information, just as you would take notes in class.

I don't take a lot of notes in class.

As you move up the grades in school, you will have to remember information for longer and longer periods before you are tested. Without notes of some kind, trying to recall information you heard or read in September for a January exam is almost impossible.

Why not just read over my textbook again?

Research shows that simply rereading the same material at the same speed in the same way you read it the first time is a poor way to study. If you read slowly, rereading is an even more ineffective and inefficient way to review. If you understood the material initially, you need only a few words or even a picture to jog your memory when you study for a test. For example, if someone shows you a picture of a party you went to last summer, you can suddenly remember all kinds of details about who was there and what went on. Good notes or a diagram or sketch work the same way for recalling facts that you once knew.

Taking notes is important for other reasons. The act of writing or drawing helps you focus on what is being said or what you're reading. There's no doubt about it, good notetaking is related to good test grades.

So what's the best way to take notes?

The best notetaking tactic is the way that's right for you, based on whether you are listening to or reading the material, what the situation is, and how you learn best. Your notetaking goal is to file away information you can retrieve when you need it. The system you use for taking notes should be one that will best help you reach that goal.

Start by looking at the traditional and time-honored ways to take notes. After you decide what basic system seems right, move on to looking at options and, finally, decide what extras you want to add. Eventually, you'll discover a way to take notes just right for your needs.

The chart at the end of this chapter called "Selecting and Upgrading Your Notetaking System" will help you. Refer to the chart as the courses you take change and your needs for notes change. Continue to upgrade the notetaking system you are using.

What about talking my notes into a tape recorder?

That's okay to do at home, but you have to allow more time for studying taped notes. Most people find that they can study written notes faster than listening to taped ones. If taped notes appeal to you, however, consider investing in a variable-speed tape recorder. As your listening skills improve, you can set the machine to play at twice the normal speed. With a headset, you can listen whenever you have a few free minutes, like while you're waiting for the bathroom to be freed up at home or waiting for a ride to school.

What about typing notes directly into my computer?

Once you become fast at keyboarding, taking notes at home or transcribing your school notes is a great use for your computer. There are some nifty programs that will put your notes in whatever order you prefer. Even without such a program, you can type notes into your computer, organize them, and shift them around to give yourself a permanent record that you can use in studying for tests or writing a paper.

Now let's talk about writing more than notes on your computer.

Selecting and Upgrading Your Notetaking System

Basic System

- Write topic and date at top of paper.

- Use only the front side of paper.

- Write down only key, or important, words and phrases; don't write sentences.

- Use abbreviations and short forms:
  w/ = with   & or + = and   RE = Roman Empire
  2 = two, too, to; "2 day" or "RE soldiers 2 organized 2 b defeated."

- Organize notes by list, outline, or diagram.

- Listen for words emphasized, repeated, or written on board by teacher; in textbook, look for boldface or italics. These will be extra important words.

- Read your notes every night to maximize memory.

Other Options

- Fold paper so that left column is about 2 inches wide, right side is 6 1/2 inches. In Column 1, put key words. In Column 2, put running notes. To study, fold the right side under and ask yourself what you know about each key word—or vice versa.

- Write the notes on NCR (no carbon required) paper with one or two parts. Keep one set at home and one in your notebook. Or swap notes with one or two friends to double-check that you wrote down the important information.

- Use colored paperclips or tape flags to mark important pages. If studying the rise of the Roman Empire, use blue for information about the Roman form of government, red for facts about the empire's expansion, and so on.

Continue →

- Draw pictures to remind you of the information. When you are desperate to remember which file drawer of your mind the information is stored in, a picture can help you recall. For example, trace or sketch a map of countries in Europe that were part of the Roman Empire and write notes on its expansion inside the map.

High-Tech Extras

- Photocopy pages of special importance.

- If you're making notes from a book at home, type them directly into the computer.

- Use a database program to enter notes. Code the field so that you can sort the material/records by date, topic, subtopics, and so on.

- Take a small tape recorder into a class and record notes.

- Record your notes on tape at home and listen to the tapes before a test.

- Use a paint/draw program to design graphics into which you can write your notes, like this:

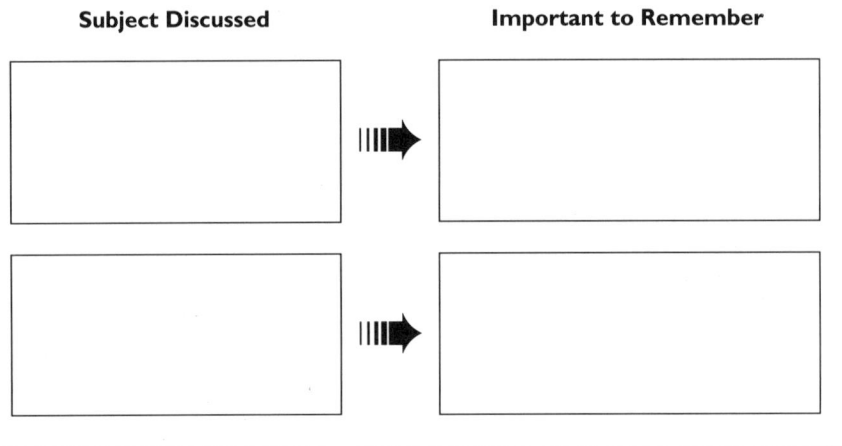

3
Getting Together What You'll Write

For many students, writing a report or even a paragraph is the hardest part of school. But writing is not a mysterious exercise in which only smart people or natural-born writers can be successful. Anyone who works at writing can improve his or her skills. The great thing about writing is that when you're done, you have an actual product to hold in your hands or to share with someone else.

You may be right, but I sure don't like to do it.
Why do you dislike writing so much?

It's a pain. You have to be so careful about how you write everything.
Perhaps it wouldn't seem like such a pain if you realize that not everything has to be written with care. Sometimes *what* you write is more important than *how* you write it. When your dad dictates a grocery list to you, he doesn't care how you spell broccoli as long as you remember to buy it, does he?

Lots of other times, what you write is also more important than how you write. In a journal or diary, you are concerned only with expressing your innermost thoughts and secrets. Or, if time is running out when you're taking an essay test, you will probably get a better grade if you pay more attention to content than to spelling every word correctly, even when spelling counts. Many teachers also encourage free writing so that students can appreciate the power of written words.

But most of the time, *how* I write seems to matter a lot to adults. I've put off writing a note to thank my grandma for a gift, because Mom taught me something like that ought to be perfect.

We suspect your grandma would like to receive a perfectly written letter from you. On the other hand, hearing that you appreciate her and what she gives you is very important to a grandma. She would no doubt prefer a note with spelling errors to not hearing from you at all!

My grandma may feel that way, but my English teacher wouldn't.

Now you are talking about what we typically refer to as *formal writing*. When you do formal writing, *how* you write is considered just as important as *what* you write. In the end, you are graded on a completed product, one that says something, is readable, and looks great.

That's a lot of work!

Formal writing *is* work—we won't try to convince you otherwise; however, we can show you a writing plan that can ease the job of formal writing.

What's the plan?

We call it the "Six C's Writing Plan." Each step in the plan starts with the letter C to help you remember it. If you follow these steps carefully, they will lead you from topic choice to final paper printout and proper presentation with the least effort and the best results.

Steps 1, 2, and 3 of the Six C's deal with *what* you write—the content and organization of what you want to tell the reader:

1. *Collect.* Collect ideas and information.

2. *Create.* Compose the paper.

3. *Cool It.* Let the paper sit awhile.

Steps 4, 5, and 6 of the plan deal with *how* you write and present your paper—how to make sure the reader will understand what you wrote, making sure you've taken out all the **bugs:**

4. *Catch the Bugs in Content.* Find and correct problems with what you said.

5. *Catch the Bugs in Conventions.* Find and correct problems with how you said it.

6. *Complete the Package.* Make your paper reader-ready.

If you use these six steps and break the big job of formal writing into small, doable bits, both the *what* and the *how* of writing will be a lot easier to accomplish.

So I'll use my computer with the Six C's?

For sure. The Six C's will help you take advantage of high tech to produce a paper you can be proud of. How much you use the computer is up to you, your situation, and your comfort level with high tech. You can, of course, adapt the steps to writing by hand if you need to.

We want to emphasize, however, that we have found some truisms about using a computer and writing, and we'd like to share them with you:

- Computers help you produce a more readable paper and encourage you to write more than you would by hand.
- The longer the paper, the more valuable the computer.
- The more complex the subject, the more valuable the computer is and the more useful other high-tech gadgets become.

Then say more about how I use the Six C's.

To explain the Six C's Writing Plan, we'll assume you are writing a paper that is about one paragraph to a page in length, in which most of the information is generated from your thoughts and ideas, but one in which both what you say and how you say it are important.

For other writing—for instance, a letter, a book report, or a fictional story—the process is basically the same. Once you understand the Six C's, you can adapt them to work for most of the writing assignments you may have. In chapter 5, we'll explain how to use the Six C's for writing longer reports and research projects.

Let's look at the first step of the Six C's. Step 1, *Collect,* tells you to collect ideas and/or information about your topic. No matter what your assignment, whether a sentence, a paragraph, or a page, you have to be interested in your topic or it will be absolutely boring to your reader! You should have some feeling, some zing, some excitement about the topic you pick.

You've got to be kidding!

No. As long as you're going to have to do an assignment, why not have some fun doing it? Think about hobbies you enjoy, TV shows you watch, trips you've taken, and sports you like.

You might think that the bigger, the better, but it's actually much harder to get a handle on too broad a topic. Choose a very small area of what interests you. If you decide to write about a favorite TV show, for example, don't pick the whole show; select one character or one episode.

But what if I'm stuck with a topic the teacher gives me?

Then at least try to work up a *little* enthusiam. You *and* your reader will die of boredom if you don't! If you don't like your assigned topic, ask if you can choose your own with the teacher's approval. If that's not an option, then try not to be negative and focus on what you'll gain from the process.

Once you've chosen your topic, start collecting the ideas you'll be using. Planning to write is like planning a trip. When you plan a trip, you have an idea about where you are going, what you are going to do along the way, and where you want to end the trip. You may not follow the plan exactly, but at least you know the general direction you'll be heading. Same thing for writing. Once you know your topic, think about what you want to say about it, how you could say it, and how you might end the piece. You may not do it that way exactly, but these ideas will help form the basis of what you write.

Should I write down my ideas?

Again, comparing writing to taking a trip may demonstrate our point. If you are just going to run down to the store for a couple of items, you scratch out a little list and head for the store. Same thing if you are writing only a paragraph or two. Jot down a few words and then go right to the second C of writing—*Create*. Plunge into writing while your ideas are hot.

But for a longer paper, as with a longer trip, you will probably want to write down your ideas and have a definite plan in mind. As you begin to think about your topic, start writing down your ideas at once. If you have ever had a brilliant thought, only to later be unable to dig it from the depths of your mind, you know the value of saving your ideas in print as soon as possible.

Do I need to put my ideas in an outline? I get all mixed up over where those capital letters and periods should be.

Only if the teacher tells you that you must. Here are some other ways to keep track of your ideas. You can:

- Write notes on cards or paper as soon as ideas pop into your head. Keep them in an envelope or folder where you can retrieve them later.

- Keep a pad of sticky notes in your notebook and put ideas on them. Since they don't go through a wash and dry cycle well, stick them on one sheet of paper or in the front of your notebook until you're ready to write—not in a jeans pocket.

- If you speak faster than you can write or keyboard, talk your ideas—either all at one time or at various moments of inspiration—into a tape recorder. Later, transcribe the tape.

Getting Together What You'll Write

- Simply list ideas or points you want to cover on a sheet of paper or on the computer.
- Use a *web,* so called because it looks like a spider's web. This web will help you map out where you are going in your writing. Jot your ideas on the ends of the web's threads, as the example shows.

Sample Writing Web

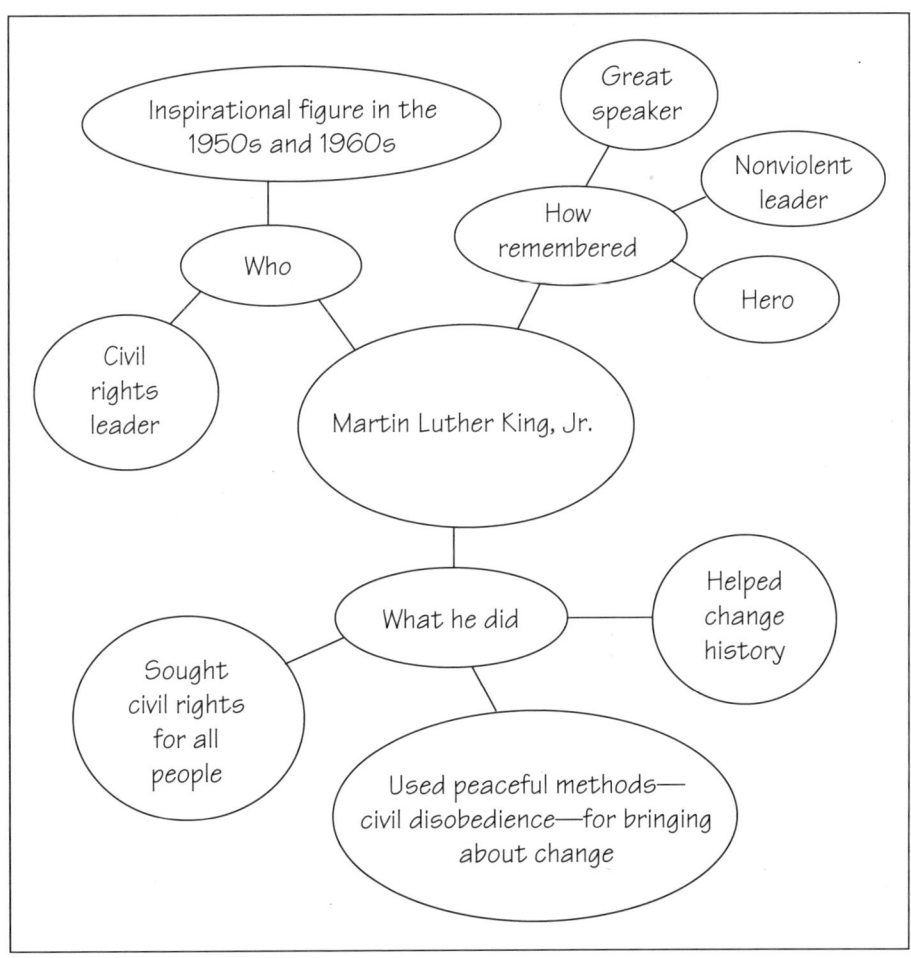

What about using a computer program to help me organize my ideas?

If you prefer a traditional outline or you have a teacher who insists that you do one, the computer can be a big help to you. Take the time to make a traditional outline format on any **word processing** program; be sure you place all the letters and numerals correctly. Save the file under a general title like "Outline Mock-up." Then, every time you need to create an outline, duplicate it and fill it in with new copy. Even though you may need to add numerals or delete letters for a longer or shorter outline, your tabs will be set, and that's the hard part.

If you prefer a web, use a paint/draw program to develop a basic one that you can duplicate.

I was talking about using a program that already has the outline on it.

Software that has various types of webs and outlines ready to be used are available and can be very useful. Some are simple and not very costly; others are extremely sophisticated and also expensive. Some of these kinds of programs are especially good for longer reports. After you answer all of the questions asked on the software, the program will then arrange your answers in a particular grouping that makes sense for the assignment you are doing. Then, T'dah!—all your ideas are organized in an outline.

So I've got my ideas in order. What now?

Move on to the second step of the Six C's, Create.

That's easy for you to say! I have a terrible time getting started.

You can't really prepare yourself to get started to create. You just have to sit down and write! Force yourself to write at least three lines about the topic. Keep writing, and your brain will kick in after a while.

Be sure, though, to keep in mind the instructions, guidelines, or rubrics (grading guide) the teacher has given you about the paper's content and its organization.

Suppose some of what I write sounds silly?

Silly is perfectly fine for beginning efforts. What if Walt Disney had thrown away his first idea of a cartoon about a talking mouse because it seemed silly?

Remember, there is seldom any single right way to write. There are many acceptable ways to present the same set of ideas.

Should I write on the computer from the very first word?

If you are still struggling to find the keyboard letters, you risk losing your train of thought as you search for each letter. You will probably feel more successful if you write by hand and then transfer what you write onto the computer.

If you're getting pretty good at keyboarding, you probably can **load** a word processing program and write from start to finish on it because creating is the step computers do best. The computer has quite literally changed the process of creating—of transferring what is in your mind into print. With a computer, you can make all kinds of changes easily—everything from a word to a paragraph, and as you become skilled, you can write almost as fast as you think.

Sometimes I write awhile and then have to stop. Getting back into writing is even harder than getting started.

Don't suddenly stop writing. Jot down some notes to cover what you will write next. Put them in a different **font** to catch your attention when you return to work. Those notes will help you get the feel of where you left off and get you in the flow of writing again. Save everything and if you are going to stop for some time, be sure to back up what you have written before turning off the computer.

We also hope you've been remembering to save as you go along with your writing and haven't been waiting until it's time to stop. As we've said before, merrily punching words into the computer without routinely saving is asking for disaster. Protect yourself and your work by saving often.

I'd better remember to save as I go along because sometimes I have a hard time thinking of enough to say as it is.

Many people have that problem, especially with certain topics. Suppose your teacher tells you to write a paragraph about what you did over the weekend. You may be able to think of only this much to say at first:

> *Sunday was a great day. I played tennis with my grandparents and played a good game. I had fun playing tennis.*

But what you write would be more complete, not to mention more interesting, if you told what made the outing special. Do you think your teacher might like this version better?

> *On Sunday, I played tennis with my grandparents. We were the first people on the courts. My grandfather taught me a better way to hold my racket and*

it must have been right because I played better than ever before. After the last game, we went to their house for lunch and we had homemade cherry pie for dessert. What a great day!

To think of more ideas for a paragraph or a paper, picture yourself telling your best friend all the details. Then expand your paper.

Two-sentence-paragraphs-with-as-little-as-possible-to-get-by writing is elementary school stuff. Since most people find it easier to write in more detail when they use a computer than when they write by hand, write everything, even a paragraph or two, on your computer as soon as you begin to gain competence at keyboarding.

When you've finished writing, move to Step 3 of the Six C's.

What's that?

Nothing. The third step of the Six C's simply says *Cool It*.

That's cool! And it can't be too hard.

It is if you didn't finish writing until midnight on a paper that's due the next morning! If your paper is more than a page or two, let it cool off for a day. For anything shorter, do something else for an hour or two before going back to it. Don't tell yourself that this step isn't important. *It is*. If you leave the paper alone and give yourself time to forget what you wrote, you'll return to it with a fresh mind. Your eye will see where it can be improved and where your writing sounds really good. Sensing you have done a good job helps give you the desire to make your writing even better. So letting your paper cool leads to your being successful with the next three steps of the Six C's. These three editing steps deal with *how you write*.

We'll talk about each of them and how they can help make your paper reader-ready in the next chapter, but first, let's review the first three C's by thinking about the first steps in the writing process.

Check out the chart labeled "Writing—The First Three Steps" on the following page. You can use it to remind yourself that your writing will be more effective and will come easier to you if you think of it as a process that's divided into several separate steps. Use the chart to map out how you went about writing your paper, then take a few moments to consider the following things about the first three steps:

- Did you collect information from as many sources as you could?

- Did you think about how to organize your ideas before you began writing?

- Did you maximize use of the computer to make writing as painless as possible?

- How long did you let your paper cool off before you began writing again?

- What will you do differently next time to make the process of writing easier and the product more effective?

Writing—The First Three Steps

Name _____ **Date** _____

Use the chart below to make notes about how you carried out the job of writing your paper.

1 **Collect**

2 **Create**

3 **Cool it**

Learning Resources Center
University of Wyoming Libraries
Laramie, WY 82070

4
Saying It With Style

For formal writing, initially creating a paragraph or paper by using the first three steps of the Six C's is only half the job. Using the last three steps to edit what you've created is equally important. Writing that is unclear, poorly organized with spelling errors and poor punctuation, or carelessly presented, may give the reader a different message from what the writer intended, no matter how creative the thoughts are.

In elementary school, my teachers just let us write—and praised everything we wrote.

They wanted to make you feel good about the process of writing and, certainly, writing strictly for pleasure is a fine pursuit anytime in life. We hope you do it often. Years from now, you'll be very interested and perhaps amused to read that journal you may be keeping.

But when you write to communicate with a reader, editing what you write is necessary. Before the days of printing presses, when everything was written by hand, no standard way existed for spelling many words and even simple names. Pages weren't numbered. The first words of sentences weren't capitalized, and one paragraph ran into another. Reading something almost meant translating it before the reader could consider what the writer meant. You may not love the idea of editing—but would you want to go back to those old ways if you were trying to read instructions for a test or how to construct a model?

No way!

Then let's talk about the last three steps of the Six C's Writing Plan. They can make your paper look good and read well. Steps 4 and 5 of writing—*Catch the Bugs in Content* and *Catch the Bugs in Conventions*—provide the eyes you need for editing; Step 6, *Complete the Package*, helps you polish your paper. Follow these steps and you'll turn in great work.

I have to admit that even for important papers, I don't go back and edit unless the teacher makes me.

Not many people think editing is fun. However, as you mature as a writer, you will see that, as we just said, correct editing helps get your message across. Because we wrote this book for your use as a reference book over a number of years, return to this chapter as you become more aware of how you write. You'll pick up editing ideas that you may not be quite ready to use just yet. In the meantime, some of our ideas should make editing less painful for you right now.

Let's give it a try. Since the third step of the Six C's was Cool It, I guess my next step now is to read over what I wrote.

Right. Step 4 is *Catch the Bugs in Content*. Computer programs can have bugs that keep them from working well, and most manuscripts have bugs that keep them from working their best.

When you are ready for this step, read your paper out loud. You may have to read it several times. Your goal is to be sure that what you wrote is clear and makes for smooth reading. It ought to be interesting as well.

How will I know whether it's clear and understandable when I reread it?

Answer the following questions to help you catch those content, organization, and style bugs:

- Does the beginning state what you will talk about in your paper? Is it up front? Clear and to the point? Is there no doubt about what your topic is and what your position on that topic will be? (This doesn't apply to a short story.)

- When reading out loud, do you naturally substitute a different word from the one you wrote? A change to a more natural word may be in order.

- Do you go on to explain what you promised in the beginning? Always keep a promise you make.

- Did you use transitions to make your writing read smoothly? Choppy writing doesn't cut it in a polished paper. Move from one sentence to another and one paragraph to another with words and phrases like *next, also, meanwhile, furthermore,* and *on the other hand.*

- Have you wrapped everything together in an ending that sums up what you talked about—or is the reader left hanging, wondering what point you were trying to make?

- Are the words you used throughout your paper interesting? Readers die two ways: by being left hanging, as we mentioned above, or by being bored to death. Don't kill off your reader!

Lots of times what I write sounds so boring that I don't like it myself—even if I like the topic.

Not all words are created equal! *Verbs* are the most important part of speech. Your verbs should be exciting action words. Because *nouns* are the second most important, choose exact nouns that say just what you want to say. Of these two writing examples, which would interest the reader more?

A) The small dog with curly fur ran into the road in front of the big red two-door car that was driving about fifty miles per hour.

B) The terrier bolted into the road as the red sedan hurtled toward it.

That's not even a contest—B. And I see how using those kinds of words would work in a short story. But suppose I'm writing a paragraph for social studies? That's pretty dull stuff.

Not if you use words that are as precise, interesting, and descriptive as you can make them. Here are two more examples:

A) The famous Great Wall of China is really, truly great. It was built by over 300,000 hardworking men. It was a big, big job. It took a long time to build. It was supposed to keep out enemies, but it didn't work.

B) Over 300,000 men labored to build the Great Wall of China, but despite the magnitude of the wall, it never succeeded in keeping out invaders.

I guess writing down anything that pops into my head doesn't always read well, but it helps fill up the pages if I have to write a certain number of words.

If you have to write 200 words, words that describe, like adjectives and adverbs, may pad the word count, but too many of them lead to boring writing. As you rewrite, substitute action verbs and exact nouns for the boring words. Add to your paper by expanding on your ideas, not your adjectives.

Also, check that you haven't used too many "be" verbs. Suppose you wrote the sentence, "I *was mad at* him." Change the "was mad at" to something like *"hated"* or *"could scream when I thought of."*

Make a habit of using a thesaurus, originally a book but now a part of most word processing programs. You can quickly locate words that are similar to the ones you used, but ones with more *accuracy* and *zip*. We selected the two words in italics after exploring in our thesaurus. Take a few minutes to check yours. Know the meaning of the words you use—but pick words with some pizzazz.

My friend says he has a program that will catch some of the bugs in content you're talking about.

Programs that analyze writing, often called **grammar checkers** or editing programs, can be useful, no doubt about it. They tell you all you want to know about your writing and then some. But they may not be as useful as you think. For example, some of the editing programs use terms like *dangling clause*. Most of them analyze noun-verb agreement, noun-pronoun agreement, active/passive tense, and overuse of certain words or jargon. If these terms don't make sense to you, you'll probably find that the information you get from such programs just overwhelms you. If it does, put the program away and try it at a later date when you understand more about grammar and feel more comfortable with the type of information it gives you.

You may, however, want to use an editing program to run a readability check on what you have written. It will show the grade level at which you wrote. Have you ever heard the term "reading level"?

Sure. Teachers tell parents that their kid is reading a book on such-and-such a grade level.

Right. A readability check analyzes elements in writing like average sentence length and average number of syllables per word to assign a reading level to a piece of writing. That can provide useful information to a writer.

Let's say that a student has dashed off a paper just to get it written and out of the way. Of course, you'd never do that.

Of course not. Never!

Finding that the quickly written paragraph checks out at a second-grade reading level may surprise or even shock that student! A readability check can highlight brief, immaturely constructed sentences and unsophisticated words.

How can I edit my writing if I don't use an editing program?

Ask a friend to swap papers with you. Don't revise the other person's work. Make a pencil check in the margin of the paper where something isn't clear or jot notes on little colored sticky notes and stick them at the trouble spots. If a friend isn't available, ask a parent to review your work.

Okay. Let's say my paper has a bunch of problems. Then what? Rewrite, I guess. I suppose doing it once won't take too much time.

Doing it once won't take too much time, but doing it properly *will*. If you want a first-class paper, rewriting may take more time than the initial writing did, so plan on spending whatever time you need to make the rewriting process work.

Charlie Self, a professional writer who is the author of thirty-five books and almost 1,000 articles, puts it this way: "A computer can really speed up work, so you have the option of turning out garbage in a rush, or taking the saved time and applying it to rewrites. Writing is rewriting and computers ease the chore."

There must be a better way of rewriting than starting all over, the way I usually do.

That's where a computer is magic. First, duplicate what you have written; then, be bold in trying changes on the copy. As you make each new copy, give it a new number or letter, such as "Cats #1," "Cats Version B." Otherwise, you may forget which one you were working with last and waste a lot of time trying to figure out what you have already worked on.

Move around sentences or whole paragraphs, add new words and ideas, and change those that aren't clear or complete. If you cut out a couple of sentences or a paragraph or two, don't just trash them. Save them in a file marked "Extras." Then if you change your mind later or you cut some copy accidentally, you can go back and retrieve what you initially wrote.

Trash something? I hate to throw anything away after all the trouble I took to write it!

We know the thought of tossing away good stuff is hard. We feel the same way. Like most writers, we actually trash more of what we write than we use.

Keep rewriting and reworking until you are satisfied that you have done the best writing job possible—and you feel confident that a reader will want to read what you said and can understand it.

It sounds great? Pat yourself on the back, then check out the fifth step of the Six C's.

I've forgotten what that was.

Step 5 is *Catch the Bugs in Conventions*.

Sounds good. I've heard of conventions where people blow noisemakers and run around shouting. At this point, I'm ready for that.

Don't shout just yet. The conventions we're talking about aren't quite so exciting. They refer to the mechanics of writing—punctuation, capitalization, and spelling. As we said earlier, these conventions make writing easier to read and understand. You might think of them as the traffic signals that allow the driver, your reader, to travel easily through your paper. Teachers expect you to pay careful attention to these conventions and respect the student who does so. And respect translates into a higher grade!

Here are a few basic questions to ask yourself about your writing and how well it meets conventions:

- Is the first letter of each sentence and of specific names capitalized?
- Are commas used correctly?
- Does each sentence end with the correct punctuation mark?
- If you quoted someone or used dialogue, did you enclose what was said in quotation marks?
- Is each word correctly spelled?

My dad says he uses a spelling checker that came with his word processing software.

Spell checkers are great; use one whenever you can, but be aware that you still have to make your own check. You can't rely on spelling checkers to catch every error. Spelling checkers don't check the way words are used. If you talk about a "pear" and you've typed the word "P-A-I-R," the checker won't pick up the error because you spelled a real word. A checker helps, but don't count on it to make your paper perfect. You also need to know how to spell correctly for the many times you're not writing on a computer, like during an exam.

Now is it time for noisemakers and shouting?

Almost. If you feel your paper shows your best writing effort, you're ready for the last step, Step 6, *Complete the Package*.

First, be sure you have carefully followed the guidelines from your teacher for matters such as margins, headings, and so on. A good word processing program makes formatting easy.

Next, choose a readable font for most of your paper, but then, unless you think your teacher will object, go wild with creative ways to highlight what you've written.

For longer papers, don't forget **graphics.** Add pictures, charts, maps, and so on, by using scanners, **CD-ROM** or computer software clip art, or drawing your own. Think about adding color if your printer prints in color or if you have access to one that does.

You might use a collage of clip art for the cover page. Also, look over the suggestions we make in chapter 6 for "Reinforcers" to an oral report. One of them may be just right to enhance your written report.

Finally, carefully insert your work into a protective folder. Look impressive? Great. But don't expect a good job on Step 6 to cover up shabby work on Steps 4 and 5. Whether a paragraph, a page, or a long report, teachers prefer content over cosmetic gimmicks.

Hey, I think I'm starting to get this stuff.

Good. Now, let's review the last three C's by thinking about the last steps in the writing process a little. Check out the chart labeled "Editing—The Last Three Steps" on page 58. It will help you to think of the two main processess of writing—writing and editing—as separate stages that lead to your goal—a well-written paper. Use the chart to map out how you went about editing your paper, then take a few moments to consider the following things about the last three steps:

- Did you use the computer or human help to catch the bugs?
- Did you make changes that were needed?
- Which part of the editing job do you need help with?

- What did you use to enhance your finished product?
- What will you do differently next time to make editing easier?

Using the Six C's doesn't sound too bad. Maybe I should be a writer.

Tell us that again when you're on rewrite number fifteen! But, in all seriousness, the Six C's can make formal writing a lot easier for you. When you at last hold that final product in your hands, knowing you have given it your best, you'll get a super good feeling, a feeling that you really do deserve to shout and toot your own horn.

Now let's talk about how to gather and organize the facts and information you need for a report or research paper and how a computer and other high-tech gadgets can help you with that kind of writing.

Editing—The Last Three Steps

Name _____ **Date** _____

Use the chart below to make notes about how you carried out the job of editing your paper.

4   **Catch the Bugs in Content**

5   **Catch the Bugs in Conventions**

6   **Complete the Package**

5

Backing Up the Facts

Anyone who has ever had a computer **crash** knows all too well what the term *backup* means. That person also knows the value of backups! *Back up* has a different but equally important meaning in writing. Sometimes your assignment is to back up what you write with information from several sources. Your teachers may call it a *research paper* or may give it a clever name. To be consistent, however, we'll use the term *report* to refer to any piece of writing in which you seek other sources to get the information needed to back up what you write.

Reports are enough to blow me over. I groan at the thought of having to do one.

The Six C's work well for writing a report, and high tech takes much of the pain from the process. But even before you begin, pay serious attention to the *objectives* your teacher gives you for the assignment and the *rubric,* or grading guide, that sets the standards on which your paper will be judged. Keep these in mind as you narrow your topic and work through the writing and editing process.

Because you need information from outside sources, you must allow lots of time for the first step. Locating the facts you need, taking notes, and sorting and organizing those notes require getting to work as soon as the subject is assigned. If you must select the subject about which you'll write, allocate additional time for this.

So I head for the library and ask the librarian for a couple of books?

Not so fast. Let's say you are assigned to write a paper for a joint science and language arts report. You must use material from three sources to explain that, over time, the animal of your choice has survived because it adapted to a changing environment.

We suggest you check out an encyclopedia before you check out library books. Although your teacher may not accept an encyclopedia as a source, it will give you an overview of many possible choices of animals you might select. You can consider several until you find one that especially appeals to you.

If I use an encyclopedia to check out a topic, I don't even need to ask the librarian for help.

You may not even need to go to the library. You may be able to get access to an encyclopedia from software on your computer.

Let's suppose you are in the kitchen, talking with your mom about your report. Since the walls are decorated with all sorts of farm animals, you consider them as a topic.

"But pigs are fat and boring," you tell her. "Besides, I don't know anything about them."

You boot up the computer encyclopedia to check what is available on pigs.

"Wow," you say to your mom a few minutes later. "Did you know that anthropologists say wild boars were around 36 million years ago and in the Middle East people domesticated pigs over 8,500 years ago?"

Now this topic shows promise and you probably wouldn't have considered pigs if you hadn't booted up the computer.

Pigs it is.

After you read a little more about your topic, think what information you need to write a paper on the subject. Develop some questions to guide your research. You will answer these questions in your paper. These questions are important because they'll keep you from wasting time researching irrelevant material that is not applicable. Of course, if your teacher has given you a set of questions, use them.

In our example, you would develop questions about how pigs adapt to their environment.

I guess I want to find out why anthropologists think pigs have been around so long...and if pigs are found everywhere in the world...and if pigs were in America long before Columbus. With a little time I can think of some more....

Depending on the expected length of your paper, three to six questions are usually enough at this point in your research. So let's say your questions are:

1. Why do anthropologists think pigs have been around 36 million years?

2. Are pigs found in every part of the world?

3. Are they native to America?

Those are good questions to get you started. Write them either on paper or type them directly onto your computer. Number each one, as we did. The questions provide a framework for looking up material and taking notes. The success of your paper depends on how well you answer the questions you pose. If you need to, add additional questions as you find out more about your topic.

Use the "Starting a Report" chart on the next page to guide you through the process from topic to title to questions. We've included four areas to write in the questions your paper will answer. Your paper may require fewer or more questions.

Now do I go to the library?

Yes. Libraries are a great source not only of books but also of high-tech resources that can lead you to other available information.

Make use of computerized research services. Subject searches are available from your friendly librarian. Talk over the costs with your parents before you obligate yourself.

In addition, most libraries are now hooked into a statewide system that provides access to books and **nonprint materials** anywhere within the state. Check with that friendly librarian to find out what is available and also what searches you can do at home via **modem.** In many places, if you have a modem, you may be able to tap into local library **databases** from your own computer to discover which library owns a book and whether or not it is checked out. If you find a book you need, you can reserve it and soon check it out. A small fee may be required.

Starting a Report

First, choose a topic and write it in the "Topic" box. Then choose (now or later) a title and write it in the "Title" box. Decide what you need to know about your subject. Then turn each of the things you need to know into a question, writing them in the ovals below.

Topic

Title

Question 1

Question 3

Question 2

Question 4

That's great. We get pizza delivered to our house. If those librarians are as friendly as you say, maybe they'll soon deliver books.

We wouldn't count on that. But almost. You may already be able to **access** articles at home. Many states have developed various types of databases summarizing articles that you can access by modem. Although these services aren't yet available everywhere, they will probably be coming soon to a library near you.

You can see why librarians are now called "media specialists" or something else that reflects the wide variety of information and materials, both print and nonprint, they have at hand. Their new titles reflect the new look of libraries. No longer are libraries quiet places filled with dusty old books. Many are alive with high tech for the public to use.

What if I can't find books and articles to answer those questions I asked?

There are many other resources you can use. Most of them are either free or not expensive, if you consider the time and transportation money you're saving. Here are some of the other possibilities:

- Phone 800 numbers. A wealth of information is yours for the asking. Use an 800 directory—available in many places, including libraries—or call 1-800-555-1212 to ask for the number of a specific organization.

- Interview authorities in person or on the telephone. Tape recording an interview is wise; have extra batteries and tapes on hand for emergencies. Low-cost devices are available to record phone conversations, but the law in most states says you must tell the person that the interview is being taped. If the calls are long distance, check with your parents before making the call; be aware how easily minutes pass when you're talking on a phone, and try to set up your call at a time when rates are cheapest.

- Contact authorities via **fax.** Not quite so easy as gabbing on a phone, but quick and convenient. No fax available? Many copying stores charge a nominal fee plus telephone rates for fax services. And, of course, a computer equipped with software and a compatible modem becomes a fax that will send material stored on it and receive any printed material.

- "Talk" with authorities and other students **online.** Once you have a modem, you can **post** messages (send and receive printed conversations) to other computer users by going online, that is, connecting with a **bulletin board service,** commonly known as a **BBS.**

I don't understand what you mean when you use the terms "online" and "bulletin board service."

You are online whenever your computer is working through a modem; however, the term usually refers to bulletin board services. These online services are the main roads of the "information superhighway" that you keep hearing about. You may already be aware of Internet, a global BBS. Some services are accessed through local telephone numbers. The local numbers are often free of charge, but national and international bulletin boards are reached by subscribing to commercial services such as America Online, GEnie, Prodigy, or CompuServe. Through these services, you can research any topic in the world. You can find out more about these services by getting their respective 800 numbers from the library.

Going online, however, is a decision you should make with your parents. Why? Because there is a downside to going online. For one thing, it can get very expensive very quickly. For another, when you go online, you talk with strangers about whom you know nothing. In essence, you invite the whole world into your home through your computer, and not all of these people are necessarily trustworthy folks you want in your home. You should exercise the same precautions with strangers online that you would with strangers you meet in person. As a rule, never give your name, address, or phone number to any stranger, whether online or in person. Online, you cannot even judge a person by how they appear. Be *very* cautious about what you say and who you talk to.

I see what you mean. I never thought about that before. But there sure seem to be a lot of different resources.

Below is a list of information resources that may be helpful to you in doing a report.

Information Sources

Check each source that you end up using for your report.

Printed Materials
- ❏ Books
- ❏ Newspapers
- ❏ Magazines
- ❏ Letters
- ❏ Pamphlets/Monographs
- ❏ Government documents

Nonprint Materials
- ❏ Movies
- ❏ Television
- ❏ Videotapes
- ❏ Audiotapes
- ❏ Performances
- ❏ Electronic mail
- ❏ Interviews
- ❏ Microfilm/Microfiche
- ❏ Online materials
- ❏ Computer software

Great! Now I've got lots of great information. What's next? Take notes?

Yes, but don't forget to choose a style that works best for you and for the kind of paper you're writing. Unless the teacher tells you how you must do it, you can use:

- Sheets of notebook paper, bound or unbound, for running notes, that is, notes that follow one after the other
- Notebook paper, with one idea per sheet
- Cards, size 3 by 5 inches or larger
- A computer, preferably with a database program that allows you to assign codes to a field for easy sorting later

I've always made running notes on notebook paper.

For a short paper, running notes are fine. For a lengthy report or research paper, you may get frustrated with running notes because you must constantly shuffle the pages to find the note you want. Developing a system for checking off a note after you use it helps, but other notetaking tactics work better.

What works better for a long report?

Writing only one bit of information per page, card, or database record usually works better for a long report because you simply go from card to card (or sheet of paper or record, if that's your choice) and the report will practically write itself.

Take a look at the chart on the next page labeled "Finding the Best Notetaking System" for a breakdown of the advantages and disadvantages of each method.

Finding the Best Notetaking System

Notes on Paper, Running Notes

Advantages	Disadvantages
• Accessible and very easy to carry with you	• Can be lost or dropped
• Very handy to write on regardless of source being used	• Can't organize and sort according to order of notes used in writing final paper
• Can color code each question you're answering with marker	• Light weight makes handling hard
• Readily available to show teacher progress of your work	• Writing report hard because of need to move back and forth among sheets
• Inexpensive—paper is cheap	
• Workable for short papers	

Notes on Paper, One Idea per Sheet

Advantages	Disadvantages
• Accessible and very easy to carry with you	• Can be lost or dropped
• Very handy to write on regardless of source being used	• Light weight makes handling hard
• Can be sorted and organized	• Multiple sheets can be confusing to handle
• Can color code each question you're answering with marker	
• Readily available to show teacher progress of your work	
• Easily accommodates large handwriting	

Continue →

Notes on Cards	
Advantages	**Disadvantages**
• Easy to carry with you • Handy to write on regardless of source • Easy to sort and organize • Can be easily color coded with a different color card for each question you're answering • Readily available to show teacher progress of your work	• Requires purchase of cards • Can be lost or dropped • Large handwriting requires larger cards

Notes on Database	
Advantages	**Disadvantages**
• Sitting at computer may aid concentration • Online resources are readily available • Easiest method for sorting and organizing material (unless notes are typed into word processing program rather than database) • Notes easily transferred to final paper • Can easily store notes for future reference • Easily accommodates problem handwriters • Risk of loss minimal if backed up	• May be difficult to place books near computer in a way that enables you to access information; alternative is to put notes on paper and perform additional step of transfer to computer • Must be printed out to show teacher progress of your work

Hmmm... I'll have to think about what will work for me.

Good. That's what finding your own learning tactics is about. Regardless of the system you pick, you will need to find the information for those notes and record it. Here is one way that works well with cards and can be easily adapted if you use sheets of paper or a database.

- *Use seek-and-find skills.* Read quickly until you find information directly related to the questions you are answering. For example, you may find some fascinating information on how to get a pig ready to show at a fair, but that's not relevant to your topic.

- *When you find an item of information, first record the source, then the question you are answering.* Summarize at the top left corner about the information source—the author (or, if you prefer, the name of the book or article) and the page number, or the name of the nonprint source (video, movie, interview, etc.). In the upper right corner, note the number of the question you are answering with that particular bit of information.

- *Make a brief note in your own words.* Recording notes in your own words will save a lot of time when you write your paper. Refer to the chart in chapter 2, "Selecting and Upgrading Your Notetaking System," if you need to review notetaking time-savers, such as abbreviating, using phrases instead of sentences, and eliminating unnecessary words.

Here's what a sample source card would look like:

```
Compton's Ency., Pigs (online)                    ③

Pigs brought to America by explorers & settlers—Vikings,

Spanish, English
```

Once I get all the notes I need from that source, I go on to get the other two sources I need. Right?

Don't go on to the other sources yet.

Why not?

The first time you use a source, record complete source information on a separate bibliography sheet. (For a sample, refer to the bibliography in this book called "Selected Resources.") Your teacher will explain the exact form for your bibliography, but here's the information needed for a book, regardless of the model your teacher prefers:

- Full name(s) of author(s)
- Title of material
- City where published
- Publisher
- Year published (latest year given)

Certain sources have their own special bibliographical form. Ask your teacher the appropriate form for referencing a personal or online quote, a book compiled by an editor, a book with numerous authors, a newspaper or magazine article, or other sources you use.

How many notecards should I have for a report?

We can't give you a number. That depends on many factors, like the length of the paper, your topic, the number of sources, and your teacher's requirements. We can only tell you to have enough cards—that is, enough information—to adequately answer your questions.

When you feel you have enough information, sort the cards into groups according to question. You may have added questions as you discovered more about your topic; that's great. If you didn't find adequate facts to answer a question, return to checking out sources or consider if the question is poor and should be eliminated.

I vote for eliminating it!

Why are we not surprised!

Now, put all the cards together that belong to each question. Then go back and organize the cards within each question in a logical order. If you are using cards or notepaper, we suggest renumbering the cards with a bright colored marker. If you drop the stack of cards or sheets of paper, the colored numbers will help you easily put them back in order.

If I put notes on a computer database, I guess sorting isn't a problem.

Right. But if you are using a computer, remember to be sure to not only make a backup copy but also to print out a **hard copy** of your notes. This is no time to risk losing all your work. Teachers today won't accept an excuse about a computer crashing anymore than they did the old excuses about a baby brother ripping up your work or a puppy eating it!

Am I finally ready to write?

Yes, you've finished Step 1 and collected your information. Now, move to Step 2 and begin to create.

What's the easiest way to do that?

As the earlier chart showed, one of the advantages of putting notes on a database from the beginning is being able to simply move them to your word processing program. If you made notes on cards or paper, type them into your computer now or begin to write.

As you enter all your information into the computer, make changes in wording that will make the paper read smoothly. You don't want the paper to sound choppy, as it is sure to if you simply type straight from notes, so take special care to add words and phrases that help the transition and overall flow of your paper. An example of two cards and how the information on them was used in a final paper is shown on the next two pages.

Once you finish writing, don't forget Step 3, Cool it. Let your report cool off for a day or two and then move on to the editing: Steps 4, 5, and 6. With a long report, you may find editing easier if you print out a hard copy and work from that rather than from the computer screen. If the report is very important to you, have someone read it out loud to you while you work from the screen and make corrections. Hearing someone else read your writing often helps you catch errors of content as well as errors of convention.

When you've selected suitable graphics and designed a sharp-looking cover, relax and give yourself some credit—you've done a great report!

Trevelan, p. 27   (2,3)

Thousands of swine wandered England in ancient times,

many years B.C.

| Compton's Ency., Pigs (online) | ③ |

Pigs brought to America by explorers & settlers—Vikings, Spanish, English

---

The History of Pigs, p. 2

    Thousands of swine wandered England in ancient times, many years B.C. Pigs were eventually brought to America by the early English settlers and also by the Vikings and Spanish.

1. *Review Notes.*
2. *Reinforce.*
3. *Rehearse.*

Begin the first R by looking at your notes and selecting the ones you'll use when you speak.

I'd rather write out the whole speech and memorize it.

Memorized speeches always end up sounding canned and false. If you understand your topic and have easy-to-read notes, you can give a speech that will come across much better than a memorized one.

Consider writing your notes on the computer. Print them in a large font so you can easily read them with a quick glance. If you've seen teleprompters on TV, you've probably noticed the type is very large. Clearly number the pages. Write out in full the first and last sentences you plan to say. Knowing exactly how you will start and stop will go a long way to helping your nerves.

What if I make a horrible mistake and say something I didn't mean to say? That thought makes me really nervous.

Radio and TV announcers face the same problem on a daily basis. They report that your best solution is just to keep going as if you didn't know what you said. Then people will wonder if they really heard what they thought they heard. On the other hand, if your mistake is obvious and everyone roars with laughter, smile ruefully, say a very genuine "Oops, sorry," and keep going.

Many people find it easier to get back on track by turning their eyes at once to their notes to cover nervousness. This trick is easier to carry out if you paste your printed notes on cards that you can hold in your hand or put on the podium in front of you.

If you choose to paste your printed notes on cards, adjust your margins to fit the card before you print. (Cards that are 4 by 6 inches or even larger are easy to handle.) Then staple (or clamp with a strong butterfly clip) the top left corner of the pages (or cards) so that if you drop them they won't fall out of order. Another way is to punch holes in the cards and put a clip ring through the holes.

And be sure to indicate on your notes when and where during your speech you will use your *Reinforcers*.

My what?

Reinforce is the second R. To involve the listeners and maintain their interest in what you're saying, use some reinforcers that remind listeners about the point of your speech. In other words (unless, of course, the teacher has said they can't be used), develop some props. Another benefit of using reinforcers is that you will have something to do with your hands. During a speech, they seem to miraculously multiply to three or four—none of which you know what to do with!

That's so right. I could use something to prop me up during a speech.

That's exactly what props do. Your props can be as simple as a picture of a motorcycle that you hold up or as elaborate as a video you created. The following examples were specifically suggested for the World War I biker project, but they can provide possibilities for any topic when modified:

- Find pictures that show what you are talking about. Photocopy them from encyclopedias or magazines. If you can, use a machine that lets you enlarge the picture so even people in the back of the room can see it. Perhaps you could find pictures of the motorcycles used in WWI.

- Use a scanner, if you have one or access to one, to scan a picture onto your computer and, depending on the printer you use, make a copy for everyone in the class.

- Tape music to begin, end, or illustrate a point in your speech. Tapes and CDs of almost every historical era are available. Check your library if friends or family don't have what you need. Music of WWI vintage should be easy to obtain.

- Talk to your grandparents and ask them to tell you what they remember hearing about World War I from their parents or grandparents. Tape-record their remarks; you may want to play one or two especially interesting comments during your presentation.

- If your family is connected to an online network, request someone who has information about your topic to **E-mail** you. E-mail is a way to send someone a personal letter through a BBS. Many older people are part of these networks and enjoy making a connection with young people interested in a topic about which they have direct knowledge or experience.

- Use your computer to design a time line banner to hang on the wall behind you while you speak. A motorcycle time line would interest both students and teachers who may not have much knowledge of the topic.

- Design a chart or graph that illustrates the point you're making; for example, how many bikers were killed in the line of duty compared to foot soldiers?

- Print bookmarks with an applicable picture or information. Perhaps all the important dates of World War I would help students have a frame of reference to better understand your speech.

- Make postcards, bumper stickers, or decals for class members. With the world of copiers and adhesive-backed papers, you can even give everyone a set of stamps. Print the stamp and perforate them around the edges by using a sewing machine without thread. You are limited only by your imagination and the cost of the materials.

- Check your local copy shop to get other ideas. *Be sure to check prices and understand how the pricing works before you place any order.* Many places can also make copies for you on colored paper, heavy papers, or clear plastic transparency sheets. Others offer large, iron-on transfers that you can use to make a T-shirt to wear during your speech that illustrates one of your points.

Those ideas sound really cool. I thought of another idea. I just bought a paint program. I can maybe use it to print a colored handout.

That's the idea. To do a great speech, get interested in it. Find some way to involve yourself and your listeners.

Once you have your ideas and your props, you'll need to do the third R, *Rehearse.*

My teacher last year told us to practice in front of a mirror.

That's still a good way. You can also audiotape your speech while you rehearse alone or in front of a family member or friend.

Best of all, rehearse your speech while being videotaped. When you play back the video, you'll see and hear how you look and sound. Do you repeatedly blink your eyes or nod your head or wave your hands until it looks like you have six of them?

All of us have gestures and mannerisms that we need to control if we are to be effective speakers. Seeing yourself can be painful, but it can also help you become a good speaker. Plan to get videotaped twice so that you can be encouraged by seeing your improvement the second time.

When you rehearse, don't forget to include playing your tape or passing out your handouts. Then you'll be sure that your props fit smoothly into the timing of your performance.

What about putting my whole report on videotape for the class?

Videotaping an entire report is risky unless you are skillful and experienced with the camcorder and are willing to write an accompanying script. If you are, then clear it with the teacher first and go for it. Ask the librarian in the reference section for a good book on making videos.

Whatever way you present yourself, we hope you "break a leg." We can't think of a better way to say "good luck," even in today's new high-tech world, than with that old stage cliché.

7

Anyone for Pi?

A lot of people believe that either you have math ability or you don't. To some extent, that's true. Some people seem to be born with a quick grasp of the concepts. But high tech provides very useful tools for those who are math minded as well as for those of us who feel somewhat math impaired.

The one important thing to remember in learning math is that it is like constructing a house. You have to start with a good foundation and build from there. If you miss learning certain basic skills as you go through the grades, you are sure to have problems.

I don't really know why I have trouble in math.

If you don't know why you have difficulties, ask your math teacher to give you a test that will help you discover your problem areas.

I know I'd do better in my math class if I could always use a calculator, but sometimes my teacher won't let us.

Your math teacher probably wants to be sure you have first learned those basic skills we just mentioned. He or she wants you to be able to do simple calculations without a **calculator.** You will undoubtedly find yourself in situations throughout your life when you need to make some calculations but have no calculator available.

To get some of those number basics fixed in your head, practice at home with a calculator that has an automatic constant addend or multiplier. For example, if you need to practice the 7's table, you would enter "7" x (which the calculator remembers). Then enter any number, think of the correct answer, and press the "=" button to see if you were correct. Do this for a few minutes every day. Keep your score of right and wrong answers for a week and you'll find surprising improvement.

Using calculators before you have certain math concepts firmly embedded in your brain can present another problem: How do you know if you've made a mistake with the calculator? Your teacher wants you to understand what you are doing before trusting your calculations to a gadget that can malfunction or on which you can make mistakes. Don't forget, *a calculator can't do math*. It can only respond to electronic blips. Wonderful as it is, *it does only what you tell it to do*. For example, suppose you are using a calculator to add $518,245 to $37,207. Let's say the calculator gives the answer $89,032. If you rely solely on the calculator, you will use that figure. If you understand place value and estimation, you realize the answer is wrong. It must have at least six digits in it because the first number you put into the computer had six places. You punched the wrong keys or maybe the battery is dying. Only *you* can prevent math errors!

Our teacher tells us to write out every step of a problem to prevent errors.

Teachers have found that students catch a mistake more easily when they can see the steps of a problem. Punching a wrong number into a calculator is easy to do and hard to catch unless the calculator provides a printed paper tape of your work.

Students who are less confident about their math skills should use a calculator that shows their work printed out or, alternatively, they should buy computer software that shows them the steps. They can then check that they entered the right numbers, didn't skip numbers, and followed the correct procedures to solve the problem. Reviewing basic steps for errors saves time in the long run.

But I see lots of students with calculators. When is it okay to use them?

Once you have a good grasp of math, most teachers allow or even encourage the use of high-tech help. Today's multifunction calculators offer portability and convenience that make them even more desirable than much of the specialized computer software. For many students, their programmable calculators go to and from school daily and are indispensable.

Calculators can't help me in one place that I really need help—word problems. They give me a lot of trouble.

Doing word problems is much easier if you divide the work into these two stages:

- The first step is to make sense of the words so you know exactly what you are to do and what facts you need to solve the problem.

- The second step is to decide what methods or formulas you need to work the problem correctly.

Don't let the storyline of the problem confuse you. Go through the sentences and underline the word or words that give you a command or direction, words and phrases like *how many, count the number of, solve for,* and *estimate.* Then jot down in your own words what the problem asks you to do. Finally, circle the facts you need to solve the problem.

You can practice doing word problems at home with any one of several math programs that are available for computers. Whatever your difficulty in math, there are many excellent computer programs out there that can help you. They cover everything from simple adding and subtracting drills to problems in algebra, geometry, and beyond. Some give you flash cards. Others give you games or puzzles that reinforce certain skills. Practice helps fix the numbers, the formulas, and the processes in your mind. Before you invest in any kind of software, though, do some investigating. Talk with your math teacher about whether the program will teach you what you want to learn. If your math teacher isn't familiar with the software you're interested in, ask around at a local computer store or check reviews of the software in magazines devoted to software or computers.

But suppose I find the computer program I buy too confusing anyway?

You may want to hire an older teenager or college student to work with you for a few weeks. If you don't have money to pay the teenager, offer to run an errand or do a chore, such as washing a car. If you ask your older sister, offer to do one of her household chores in exchange for her time.

I hear kids in the honors math class talking about using a spreadsheet in math. What is that?

A **spreadsheet** is a special way of doing certain kinds of problems on the computer. A spreadsheet is a way of storing and sorting data in rows and columns in worksheet form. It lets you analyze practical problems by experimenting with the various parts of the problem.

Suppose your problem is to determine which size and how many TV sets you should store in your small warehouse to make the most money. A spreadsheet would let you try out several different sizes and prices of TVs and turn that data into a graph or a table. From that graph or table, you could make your decision.

You can buy kid-friendly spreadsheet programs that teach you to crunch numbers like a pro. Using such programs, you can convert recipes, calculate sports statistics, and even begin to get into advanced math functions. You may want to use them for personal projects as well as school assignments. You could also keep records and do studies on pets, diet, sports, and even where your money goes!

You could, for instance, keep track of your physical fitness scores, like the number of push-ups or sit-ups you do or how long it takes you to run a mile. And, of course, you can keep data on your attendance at school and your grades. Teachers do make mistakes, you know, and having the data to back up a point of disagreement might be useful!

My dad says if my sister wants to be a scientist, she'll need to learn how to use a spreadsheet.

He's right. But scientists use computers for a lot more than spreadsheets. Science research has changed dramatically since the computer has become common in science labs. Most scientists do all of their work on computers, swapping information with each other online.

Although your sister isn't a scientist yet, there are many fascinating science programs that she can use now that are available for computers. In all likelihood, she'll use these on school computers because they are often very expensive.

On the other hand, whether you want to be a scientist or not, you can do some really neat science projects just with the computer you have, if you have a word processing program that lets you make tables or if you have one of the spreadsheets we just talked about.

Suppose you want to keep tabs on the weather to prove to your cyberspace pen pal that the weather is worse where you live than it is where she lives. Make a chart on your computer and, by using low-cost weather instruments, you can keep daily records of temperature, wind speed, and rainfall or snowfall totals.

If you exchange charts and weather information online every day, you can begin to do a little weather forecasting. For example, you may soon be able to predict pretty accurately how long it will take a storm that is west of you to begin dropping rain in your yard.

That's pretty cool, but I really like growing things even more. What could I do on my computer to help grow bigger and better plants?

You can keep records of planting dates, how seeds or seedlings were planted, fertilizing schedules, blooming dates, and harvesting times. Soon you will know how to grow the healthiest plants in your neighborhood.

The best part is that you can turn these fun projects into reports for your science or other classes. For a more sophisticated report, you may want to check out software that lets you add charts, diagrams, and illustrations to your paper. Check on your BBS to see if someone else with the same interests as you has already developed charts or software programs that you can use. Don't forget to always use a **virus checker** on your computer if you download any **shareware**.

Maybe I could do better in the science fair this year if I worked up a science project on my computer. I bet I'd have more fun, too!

Sure, and if you need more help about your topic, there is even software designed to help you choose a topic and develop it for a science fair.

Is there any other high-tech equipment that would make schoolwork easier or more interesting for me?

Many people feel that you ought to upgrade your equipment and get a CD-ROM for your computer as soon as your family feels it can afford one. This is hardware that lets you see both text and images on your monitor as if you were viewing a movie and reading a book at the same time. You can look up a topic and see text or related pictures and hear the accompanying soundtrack with all of it under your control. Already CD-ROM publishers have produced encyclopedias, atlases, and foreign language materials in this form as well as materials on history, music, nature, and a variety of fun topics.

Gee, things change so fast. How can I stay up with what's new and useful in computers or software?

On your next birthday, ask for a subscription to a good computer magazine that appeals to you. Check out several of them on a newsstand. There are magazines for beginners, magazines for families, and magazines for the really superskilled. New products are advertised and reviewed in these magazines. The editors screen out bad software and discuss only the best. Most of them grade these better programs, and the reviews can often help you select the programs that are right for your needs.

Another source of information about new products are the fairs and expositions put on by major computer manufacturers. Someday soon in the big city nearest you, there will be a computer fair or conference. Watch for an advertisement in your local paper or ask around at your local computer store. A visit to one of these big events can give you an eye-popping view of the high-gadgets yet to come and others that have already arrived.

User groups are another source of information. Each brand of computer has local clubs that can fill you in on upcoming products and answer questions about equipment and software you already own.

I don't think I'd want to sit around with a bunch of adults. I'd feel dumb.

If you don't want to belong to an adult user group, consider joining a computer club at school or, with the help of a friend, forming one in your neighborhood. When a group of people who are interested in the same equipment put their heads together, they can help each other learn and discover all kinds of new ways to apply their knowledge and expertise, both at home and at school.

Once you decide to use your computer for more and more of your studies, you and your computer will make a great team, no matter what you are interested in doing or learning.

Learning is one thing. Testing is another. If only we didn't have tests, I could like school a lot more.

Then let's look at how a computer can help you ace those tests and not worry so much about them.

8

Taking a Byte Out of Tests

To ace a test, you first have to know the material. If you do, you feel confident, and confidence is necessary for test success. But most students are not sure how to go about learning the material well enough to be confident and are not sure how to use what they do know in the test situation.

To do your best on a test, you need to be testwise. To become testwise, you need to:

- Adapt the way you study for different types of tests
- Understand the different kinds of tests
- Develop your own strategy for taking tests

Why should I change the way I study for different types of tests?

You'll save time and effort if you focus your energies on the kinds of information the test will require. Do you need to think about main ideas for essay-type questions? Or will the questions be true-false so that you need to study primarily facts and details? Or will there be lots of short answer questions so that you need to memorize many items?

I don't see why I have to clutter up my mind with lots of dates and facts when I can store them on a computer and look them up whenever I need them.

In time, schools will change and testing will change. When pocket computers become as common as calculators, facts won't be the main point of testing. Teachers won't be asking students to remember material they can access quickly, but until that time, traditional testing will prevail.

So how do I find out if I have to memorize all that stuff?

Ask. Sometimes teachers will tell you, sometimes they won't. You are most likely to get an answer if you phrase your question properly. If by tone of voice or words you sound as if you are trying to wheedle the test questions out of the teacher, the teacher will most likely refuse to answer you. Instead, ask politely if you should put more emphasis on memorizing details or looking at main ideas or thinking about relationships. That asks for a focus, and the teacher may tell you what type of test to expect.

If the teacher won't tell you, use your wits. Think about what seems important to that teacher. What kinds of tests has the teacher usually given? What kinds of questions does he or she ask students? Are the questions about details or about general ideas? Does the teacher tend to talk about main issues or are the teacher's lessons full of facts and figures?

Teachers act weird about tests. They want you to do well, but some act as if they want the testing to be a secret.

Testing is always a problem for teachers. Their job is to teach you.

The primary way to tell if they have succeeded is to test you. But unless your school tells teachers what tests to give, each teacher decides for him or herself when and how often to give tests and what kinds of tests to give. Here are some of the reasons why you get such a variety of tests:

- Many teachers make up their own questions. Such a teacher tests the way he or she teaches. Sometimes a student who is a year ahead of you can tell you if that teacher asks for lots of short answers, uses multiple choice, or asks students to think about and analyze problems. Knowing generally what kinds of questions a teacher asked in the past will give you clues about what to expect.

- Some teachers take their tests directly from the questions at the end of a chapter or from the test questions at the back of the book. Ask your teacher if test questions will come from the book's questions. If the teacher won't tell you, you will know after your first test, since most teachers follow the same pattern the rest of the year.

- Teachers usually make up essay questions themselves. The more students the teacher teaches, the less likely the teacher is to use lots of essay questions because they take longer to evaluate and are harder to grade than objective tests.

- More and more teachers are now constructing tests from software they buy or from computer disks that are sold with textbooks. If the tests are machine or computer graded, they tend to contain lots of factual questions and not a lot of essay questions.

Computer banks of tests, called **test banks,** can work to your advantage, however. For example, if you really mess up an exam, your teacher may allow you to study and retake the exam because a bank of questions makes a new exam on the same material easy to give and grade.

Suppose I have an idea of the kinds of questions that will be on the test. I guess I just start studying and work until I fall asleep.

That's not smart. Study for about twenty-five minutes and then take a five-minute break. You'll return to your studying with a fresher mind and be better able to do the thing that is most important while you are studying—concentrate. Many students who find studying boring are not concentrating on the task. *Stay focused.* If you have a problem, deal with it, then go back to your studies. Of course, dealing with a problem does not mean spending two hours on the phone talking with a friend about a party!

To maximize your study time and ability to learn more, read material initially and then review it right before a test. If you wait until the night before a test to read a chapter for the first time, you will have a harder time remembering it the next day than if you have read it at least once before.

Studying for a test should be mostly a matter of reminding yourself of important details and points. Go over summaries of chapters and read through your notes. If it is a math test, go over simple examples of each kind of problem.

What about listening to music while I study?

You may focus better if you listen to classical music—yes, classical, as in Beethoven. Research shows that complex music helps many students retain complex information. Simple rock, rap, and other styles apparently don't have the same effect.

What about cramming?

Use cramming only to remember facts, such as dates and names. However, one of the best ways to study for other kinds of information is to make up good sample questions and practice answering them. If you study with a friend, each of you can make up questions, swap questions, and check how well you do.

How do I know if the test questions I make up are good?

Make up questions that use words printed in bold-faced print or italics in your textbook. They are almost always main ideas or important facts, such as the event that started a war, an important theory, or basic experiments and their outcomes. As you read, jot down the word or phrase and page number whenever you come to an idea that you would use on a test if you were testing the other students in your class.

We can't write in our books.

Attach any sticky note or tape flag next to the idea.

Where does my computer fit in?

As you go back through the book, make up a question and type it into the computer. Skip several spaces and then type in the answer. When you are ready to test yourself, pull up the first question so that it just shows at the bottom of your screen. Try to answer the question, then scroll up to see if you were correct. Move on to the next question. Turn this into a game with a friend to see who can answer the most questions the other person wrote.

If you're studying for a math test and you have math software, load comparable problems and test yourself. There are good computer programs for foreign language review, too. If taking tests is a super big problem for you, consider investing in a high-quality computer program on test taking. These programs let you print study lists and help you review materials, and much, much more.

You can also use your computer to make and print flash cards for drill. Print the whole sheet of paper and then cut it apart. Use flash cards for studying vocabulary, which, incidentally, is a great way to learn words of a foreign language.

You might use the smallest legible font to type out on one sheet the most important facts needed for the test. Voilà! You'll get a big psychological boost from having everything you need to study on one sheet. Tucking a single sheet into a pocket to study when you have a few spare minutes on the school bus is also easier than yanking a large textbook out of your backpack.

You might also check if test banks are available online. **Download** tests in your subject and use them for prepping.

Any suggestions for taking the test itself?

You probably already know the general points. Study well, get a good night's sleep, eat some breakfast, especially if you have a morning test. If your test is in the afternoon, eat a light lunch. Pass up the heavy, greasy foods that may make you sleepy about test time. As with other learning tactics, however, every successful student develops his or her own style of test taking.

If tests make you anxious, avoid talking or listening to other people. Whether they feel good about their studying or are afraid they'll do poorly, listening to them can make you nervous.

When you take the test, relax, draw a deep breath and then *carefully read any instructions*. Don't just jump in and start to work and later find you have wasted your time.

Estimate how much time you have to complete each part of the test and begin. Don't spend too long on a hard question. On the other hand, don't rush through the test because you are eager to go on to something else.

Students who can't rely on short-term memory often like to jot down items or lists they have memorized before the facts fly from their minds. Other students prefer to answer all the easy questions first.

Be on the lookout for a question that contains clues to help you answer another question.

In summary, take into account your own personal strengths and weaknesses. Experiment until you find the most effective way for *you* to study and the most effective test-taking tactics for *you*.

What about taking machine-graded tests? I'm not as neat as I might be and I mess those up sometimes.

You have to be extremely careful answering **machine-graded** tests. A machine grades what it "sees," not what you want it to "see."

The big mistake most people make is getting confused and putting an answer mark on the wrong line. Every answer that follows is then wrong. Here are several hints to help you:

- Use a small ruler, a flat-sided pencil, or any other small straight-edge to be sure you put the mark on the same line as the number of the question.

- Using your straight edge, carefully answer questions 10, 20, 30, 40, and so on first. Then go back and work through the test from the beginning. Completing every tenth question means your tracking won't be off by more than nine.

- Each time you answer a question, use a blunt, dark pencil and make a single strong mark across the middle of the circle or square. Buy a fat primary pencil; that kind works well to save time while filling in the space with only one stroke. Don't bother to fill in the entire space. All the machine is looking for is a dark spot. If you make a mistake, carefully erase every bit of your mark, or the machine may select the wrong dot. Also, be sure to erase any stray pencil marks from the answer sheet.

One of my friends goes to a private school where they don't just grade tests by machine, they give tests right on the computer. He says it's almost fun. That's hard to believe!

Some schools are using a completely different kind of testing these days, thanks to the computer. Here's how it works: The teacher writes a hard question, a middling question, and an easy question for every topic. If you miss the hard one, the computer will tell you and will automatically give you the easier question. If you miss that one, the computer will give you the easiest question. When you finish the test, you and the teacher will know not just whether you got a question right or wrong, but also how well you really understand the topic or concept.

My sister said her driver's license test was given on a computer.

Right. That's another reason for becoming very familiar with a computer for test taking. More and more licensing tests and tests for job applications are given on computers.

There's no doubt about it, you will live in a high-tech world in the twenty-first century. As you read this book, scientists and engineers are hard at work developing even more amazing kinds of equipment that will be in place in the working world by the time you graduate.

9
Your Place in High Tech

In this book, we've looked at a lot of ways that high-tech equipment can help you meet the challenges of a new information age. We hope we gave you some ideas that you started using the moment you read them. But even more important, we hope we've started you thinking about how you can modify the ideas in this book to develop even better learning tactics in the future. Remember that you're a unique individual, and you need special learning tactics that are uniquely yours, both now and as you move through life. To make the most of high tech and what we've discussed in this book, you can continue to find your own best ways to:

- Keep track of assignments.
- Organize and remember what you read and hear.
- Take notes.
- Use the Six C's Writing Plan for formal writing and take advantage of a word processing program as you collect ideas and information, create, cool your writing, catch the bugs in content and conventions, and complete the package you've created.
- Relax and take what's useful from the Six C's for informal writing.

- Research a subject about which you need information by utilizing the multitude of resources in varying media forms.
- Develop techniques for talking in front of a group by making notes, reinforcing what you say with props, and rehearsing your presentation.
- Develop and learn math concepts and use basic math facts.
- Adjust the ways you study and take tests.

Some of the things we've talked about, however, may not be really helpful to you until you're older and have your own personal computer and some of the other gadgets we've mentioned. Keep this book handy as you move through school and refer to it as you continue to learn about how you learn. As your assignments become harder and more complex, use the handy "Quick Reference Guide" in this book to upgrade your skills in reading, writing, editing, researching, math, and test taking. Just as you want to regularly upgrade to the fastest, most powerful computer you can afford, you should also constantly upgrade your learning tactics to help your brain work as fast and powerfully as it can and to make the most of the available technology.

Because there is always ongoing research, you will need to stay alert to new information and new technology. Scientists and engineers are constantly building new kinds of computers and are busy paving the information superhighway. Educational researchers are always looking at how we learn and the ways we take in information and retrieve it, whether through print form or through visual images. If you continue to upgrade your learning tactics, you will be ready to incorporate each new idea as it becomes useful to you.

Don't forget that, although more awesome and exciting new products are just a discovery away, no one anytime soon will develop any technology as great as your very own brain. Save yourself time and energy by using high-tech equipment for routine tasks. Then use your remarkable brain to do even higher level thinking and create a wonderful life for yourself and others. You can do it!

Selected Resources

This list of resources uses *The Chicago Manual of Style* bibliographical forms. The entries, from first to last, represent the following types of sources: E-mail, magazine article, book, personal interview, fax letter, book, BBS post, and newspaper article with author.

AFC Tooter. *Re: Help! again clarified.* E-mail to MaryB8, 94-04-07 22:56:29 EDT.

Crisci, G. "Discover and Create." *Kids & Computers,* December, 1992, pp. 38, 56.

Fleischman, P. *Copier Creations.* New York: HarperCollins, 1993.

Garr, D., and M. Garr. Interview by C. G. Wirths and M. Bowman-Kruhm. Tape recording. Potomac, Md, 29 January 1994.

Old, W. *Maryland Libraries' System.* Fax to M. Bowman-Kruhm, 8 October 1993.

Schwartz, P. *How to Make Your Own Video.* Minneapolis: Lerner Publications, 1991.

Self, C. *"Writing on a Computer,"* America Online [electronic bulletin board], 94-02-25, 14:53:47 EST.

Span, P. "Women and Computers: Is There Equality in Cyberspace?," *The Washington Post Magazine,* 27 February 1994, pp. 10–13; 23–26.

Acknowledgments

We would like to thank the following people for their help: the students at St. James Episcopal School, Hagerstown, MD; Jim Probasco, Columbus (OH) Public Schools; student consultants David and Matthew Garr; Rosemary Garr, Montgomery (MD) County Public Schools; Darryl Norwood, Montgomery (MD) County Public Schools; Robert Capels, Carroll County (MD) Public Schools; Rose Mattaui, Carroll County (MD) Public Schools; Dr. Richard Mainzer, Millersville University; Pat Perrin; Wendie Old; Charlie Self; Audrey Hill, Montgomery County (MD) Public Schools; Marcia Vandermause; and Elinor Zevin, Montgomery County (MD) Public Schools.

Additionally, we would like to thank the following people for their special assistance: Karen Dowling, Professional Library, Montgomery County (MD) Public Schools; Bonnie McComb, Montgomery County (MD) Public Schools; and Emery Roth II, Region #12 Public Schools in Connecticut.

Glossary of High-Tech Terms

Access
To gain entrance.
She was able to *access* the **file** that listed college entrance requirements.

Audiobook
Any book read on audiotape; may be complete or condensed.
To help review long and difficult works, he liked to listen to *audiobooks*.

Backup/ back up
A noun that means a copy of what you have written on the computer; a verb that means to make a copy of your work, usually on a floppy **disk** or a tape.
To be certain that her work was saved, she kept a current *backup* of essays. She routinely would *back up* her files every fifteen minutes to keep from losing them.

BBS
Abbreviation for Bulletin Board System.
He frequently exchanged suggestions and ideas with others on a *BBS*.

Boot up
To start up the computer.
She made it her habit to *boot up* her family's computer every day after school.

Glossary of High-Tech Terms

Bug
Something that causes a problem with what you are trying to do.
Every time she tried to use her friend's **program,** new *bugs* would cause her computer to flash error messages.

Bulletin Board System
A computer system that allows users to communicate with one another by posting messages; for example, Internet, America Online, CompuServe, GEnie, and Prodigy as well as thousands of local ones.
Once he joined a *bulletin board system*, he could communicate by computer with his older sister in France.

Calculator
A machine that does math functions; a programmable calculator allows input of frequently used formulae.
He feels much more confident now that he can use a *calculator* to check his math problems.

CD-ROM
A compact disc (read-only memory for storage) that is displayed on a computer monitor.
Ever since her family got an encyclopedia on *CD-ROM*, she has made fewer trips to the library.

Clip art
Pictures, cartoons, and diagrams available for general use on a computer program.
He decided to make his presentation more exciting by creating handouts that had *clip art* on them.

Crash
Noun or verb that means any part of computer **hardware** or **software** that suddenly ceases to work.
Her paint/draw **program** used so much memory that it kept making her computer *crash*.

Glossary of High-Tech Terms

Cyberspace Imaginary world of electronic information.
He knew he needed to save the illustrations he made for his report or they would disappear into *cyberspace*.

Database A computer collection of information that can be searched quickly.
She typed in the subject for her report on the library's *database*, which then displayed a list of possible resources.

Disk Circular plastic platter, sometimes called a floppy disk, on which data can be stored.
He would copy his drawing **files** onto a *disk*, then take it to a copy shop where he would print them out in color.

Download The transfer of stored information from another computer to make it available to your computer.
She would often *download* **E-mail** from the **BBS** and read it later.

E-mail Electronic mail sent from one computer to another.
She felt that sending messages by *E-mail* was a lot easier than mailing letters.

Fax Widely used abbreviation for facsimile to indicate an exact copy transmitted via telephone lines.
Sometimes when she needed information right away, she would ask people to *fax* it to her at the corner copy shop.

File A collection of information on a disk that you call by one name.
He decided to call the *file* with his essay on it "Reader Beware."

Find function The capability of a computer to locate **files** or a word stored in its memory.
He had lost his file named "Mom," but found it when he used the *find function.*

Font A complete set of characters of one size or style.
She could easily make her handout more appealing by printing the title in a fun-looking *font.*

Grammar checker A program that analyzes the grammar, punctuation, readability, and style of a document. Also called an editing program.
He decided to ask his friend to read his paper, just in case his *grammar checker* missed any of his mistakes in usage.

Graphics Any computer-generated symbols and shapes, such as bar, pie, and line charts. Also, pictures in general.
She wanted to add some *graphics* like bar charts to illustrate her report on the methods of transportation most commonly used.

Hard disk A disk drive that contains large amounts of memory.
She added a new *hard disk* to her computer before she wrote her book so she would have enough memory for all of her files.

Hard copy Computer information that has been printed.
Since he found it hard to read his paper from the computer screen, he also printed out a *hard copy* of his report to work from.

Hardware The actual machinery of the computer.
She now had all the computer *hardware* she needed, but still kept hoping her parents would get a color **monitor.**

Glossary of High-Tech Terms

Input
Entering information into the computer.
His friends were waiting outside his house, but before he left for the beach he wanted to *input* the rest of his short story.

Keyboarding
Typing on the computer's keyboard.
Since she took that *keyboarding* class over the summer, she'd been able to type up all her work in a flash.

Load
Putting a **software** program onto a **hard disk**.
Before he could use the new paint **program** he got for his birthday, he had to *load* the **software.**

Machine-graded
An electronically scored test.
She was relieved to know that their exam would not be *machine-graded*, since she much preferred essay exams.

Modem
A device that uses telephone lines to allow computers to talk to each other.
Now that her family had a *modem*, she frequently used it to leave messages for her older brother on his computer at college.

Monitor
The computer screen and the box around it.
He carefully measured the distance between the *monitor* and where he sat to do his work.

Nonprint materials
Any source of information not printed; for example, movies, TV, CDs, and audiotapes.
For her oral presentation, she used a variety of *nonprint materials*, especially audiotapes of recorded interviews.

Online
Connecting your computer to a telephone/modem to allow you to communicate with other computers or access a **BBS** or online computer service.
His report would include several sources that he found out about through an *online* computer service.

Paint/draw program Computer software that allows you to draw and paint.
She created some signs for her school's fundraiser using her new *paint program* to add graphics.

Post To write a message onto a bulletin board.
He would *post* a message on the **BBS** that he was available to tutor students learning German.

Printer A device that converts data in a computer to letters and numbers on paper.
The new color *printer* at the library would allow him to print a fun cover sheet he had made using his **word processing** program.

Program A collection of instructions that tells a computer what to do.
Her father told her that she must look at reviews of the math *program* to see what it could do before she could get it.

Save A command you give your computer to store your work.
Because he'd lost several papers he had written, he learned to tell the computer to *save* his work every few minutes.

Scanner A device for copying print and photographs into a computer.
For her report on conservation, she would try to use a *scanner* to add a photograph of an old-growth forest to her computer file.

Glossary of High-Tech Terms

Screen saver
A **program** that causes words or pictures to appear on the screen when the computer is on but not in use.
They had a new *screen saver* in the computer lab that showed an image of a leaping frog bouncing across the computer screen.

Shareware
Software usually found on a **BBS** at little or no cost.
She was careful to send money for the *shareware* she used.

Search
To hunt for.
He used the library **database** to *search* for information on Steinbeck.

Shut down
Turn off.
The computer would bark every time you went to do a *shut down*.

Software
A program or a collection of programs containing instructions to a computer to perform a series of tasks.
They had only one piece of *software*, the one that came with the computer.

Spell checker
A program that analyzes spelling.
She relied on the *spell checker* to find all her errors in her paper and didn't read through it carefully before turning it in.

Spreadsheet
A form of storing and working with data in rows and columns in worksheet style. Also used to describe software programs that create spreadsheets.
Over the summer, his mother took a class that taught her how to use *spreadsheets*, so he hoped she could show him what she learned.

Test bank	A **database** of questions. Her make-up exam would already be available tomorrow, since her science teacher used a *test bank* to put together the exam.
Virus checker	Software that scans computer files to check for destructive programs. He found a *computer virus* entered his files when he borrowed a friend's disk.
Word processing	A noun that means computer program for writing; an adjective that describes a specific program. The first **program** she used was a *word processing* one that her dad used for writing letters.